Co-Authors

Kajal Hemal Mehta

Invincible Publishers

First Printing: 2019

ISBN: 978-93-89600-19-3

Invincible Publishers

Registered Address: 201A, SAS Tower, Sector 38, Gurgaon - 122003

Dedicated to all the readers who have showered my first book ***'Just One More Button Down'*** *with immense love and praises; and to you who is holding this one.*

Such love, appreciation and warmth is my inspiration to continue this journey as a writer

Acknowledgement

This one is to my parents for raising me to be what I am, though I haven't stopped giving them hard time.

This one is to my husband who has made me spread my wings and look up to the sky, no matter what.

This one is to my son, who has grooved himself with my demanding life; to him, for his unconditional love.

This one is to my sister for all her love, support and care throughout the years and many more to come.

This one is to my in-laws for agreeing to the fact that I have my dreams and letting me try to make them real.

This one is to my friends who remind me everyday that I am loved just the way I am.

This one is to each one out there who is my support system, who I know will cushion me and not let me fall.

This one is to each senior person from the fraternity who believe in me and make my journey as a writer so powerful so that I will go on writing forever.

And this one is to those angels who don't wear golden ring and a white robe, nor do they fly; who just act to be one of us, but I know they are angels.

Thanks to All.

Table of Contents

Chapter 1

'Hi Marshmallow! How are you today?' Jiya smiled, loving the way this small note made her feel.

'I am as good as your sweetness could make me feel.' She typed back.

Jiya got out of the bed and walked towards the mirror. She did not like her shabby look, but she knew that Ronit would love that first morning click. She grabbed her phone stuck between her skin and the elastic of her pajamas. A warm thought of Ronit tickled her when her fingers touched her skin just below her waistline and she blushed. Stepping away from her comforts, she gave her best angles and tried to grab a good morning selfie for Ronit. She suddenly realised that it was already 15 minutes since she had the phone in her hand, and she was getting late. She turned the camera off and quickly sent one click that she thought was the best. She opened the music folders in her phone and opened a folder titled 'Bath Time', which was her bathroom companion. This folder was loaded enough to accompany her during the 45 minutes that she usually spent every day in the bathroom. But after much pondering, Jiya could not settle on her everyday favorites, shuffling around for other songs to make her feel more romantic. Surfing through her collection of around 325 songs did not satisfy her and she felt irritated. She wasted some more time to settle on what she wanted to listen to.

'What kind of music do you like?' She drafted a message to Ronit but did not send it.

Jiya's mind was throwing her back in the past without her consent. There was something about today that made her miss him this bad.

She missed the time when she did not have to worry about sending any messages to him. In fact, thinking before speaking was considered as a crime in their never talked about 'rule book'. She was lost in the thoughts of old times in the warm bubble dip and missed a few mild knocks at the door of the bathroom. A slightly louder than usual knock broke her chain of thoughts.

'Shall I serve your breakfast? I think you are running late.' It was Sita, her maid who had worked in their house since her childhood. Jiya is the daughter of a well-heeled family; her father is a rich man, who has made his fortunes working hard in the construction industry. His business is spread mostly in the Asian and Gulf countries. Jiya, being the only child of this family, is coddled much typically. She has a degree in interior designing from one of the best designing schools of India. As her interviews read, she claims that she could have gone to any of the top international schools to get a degree, but she believes that experience is the best school; and the growth of her career is proof of it. She started her career with small projects like designing small apartments, and today she designs not only penthouses of the HNIs and NRIs, but also hotels and resorts.

'I work as an interior designer to feed my body and other materialistic needs. But I write to feed my soul.' She once told during one of her interviews. This remained unnoticed until she started her own blog and started building her fame real soon. Many praised her writing more than she thought she deserved. She was aware of all such characters and their intentions behind the board praises. She wore branded clothes, watches, shoes and bags. She drove fancy cars which complimented her good looks, confident persona and rich-by-birth identity. She came across a few people and incidents claiming her splendors were results of her father's behind the scenes influence. Jiya never cared to justify; she was a woman of substance who believed that she was not answerable to people to change their ideas about her. She just looked up and continued walking on the path she had designed for herself.

She stepped out of the floor leaving puddles of water on the floor and opened the door slightly ajar, 'Oh yes, Sita mata.' Sita has been raising Jiya since she was an infant. She knew Jiya's likes, dislikes, emotions, goals, and everything else like a mother would need to know to raise her child. Sita's love for Jiya was absolutely motherly.

Sita looked at Jiya's reflection in the mirror through that ajar door and found her doll had grown up to become an envious woman. Jiya's curves made Sita feel proud and worried at the same time about her little girl. She would be able to impress any man she would develop fondness for, but what if someone played with her emotions just because he was smitten by her boons.

Jiya was dressed in a pink shirt tucked in her khakhi trouser, perfectly paired with a brown belt, shoes and a handbag to go with as she appeared at the breakfast table.

Her impeccable dressing and articulately applied make up spoke volumes of her self-awareness. She exchanged her morning pecks with her parents and smiled at Sita when she caught her looking appreciatively at her. She blew her a kiss in the air.

As she picked up her perfectly toasted toast and took the first bite, her mind took her on ride to the past. It was the same morning when it had all begun. She was sitting on this same table with her parents that morning.

* * *

'Mom, dad, I am going to Jaipur tomorrow for a book festival.' Jiya announced.

'Book festival? Since when have books started interesting you, Ginnie?' Her father loved calling her with this name, and Jiya loved it equally.

'You hardly have time to notice her growing interest in writing. She writes well, few of her stories have even won some prizes. She has a decent amount of fan following on her blog too.' She was not sure if her mother was being sarcastic about his absence at home or was sharing achievements of their daughter out of sheer excitement.

'So, when are you flying to Jaipur? Do you want me to book the tickets or have you booked them already?' Her father was extremely protective about her. He had availed high riches and had no issues spoiling her with worldly goods.

'I am going by bus, Papa. I have some friends from the local book club going there, and a bus is already booked for us. I will be good, don't worry.' Jiya was very excited about this new travel mode in the company of likeminded people.

'I don't approve of this. You are Jiya Juneja–daughter of Tejas Juneja. You cannot be travelling by bus! I hope I make myself very clear.' Tejas Juneja was disturbed with the developments taking place in the house against his high standards, especially without his knowledge, leave aside approval.

Jiya's mother looked at her, silently signaling her not to argue. Jiya kept mum understanding her mother's indication. His father took her silence as a white flag and instructed his staff to coordinate with Jiya to book her flight tickets. By evening Jiya had her tickets. Her father's discomfort seemed to have subsided too, and an offer to go on a drive and have ice cream was a sign of his better mood.

'No matter what mumma, I am not flying to Jaipur. I want to get acquainted with people from that world and portraying that I am a princess will never let me get close to them.' Jiya was adamant. Kinnary – Mrs. Tejas Juneja was looking at Jiya with a surprised look. Jiya's maternal family was equally influential just like the Junejas, however, right from the day they got married, Tejas made sure to stamp his dominance over the relationship. Eventually, Kinnary adopted his priorities, lifestyle and looked after the family just the way he wanted her to.

'Being independent is good Jiya, but don't try to overrule your father. He won't like it. He is just trying to give you more comfort and being protective towards you.' Kinnary sensed something unseen in Jiya for the first time, and she feared that it would result into unnecessary stress between Jiya and her father. She tried to persuade her to go by flight but she failed.

Chapter 2

Jiya as adamant as she was this time got on the bus with her fellow members of the local book club. She liked the long hours of traveling, which meant exchange of prose, poetries and experiences from upcoming authors. Jiya tried to be a part of them by leaving her 'I am a princess' approach aside. Some people and their attitude disturbed her, but she was determined to be at the Book Fair with these people and that helped her to face everything that came her way.

The environment was completely mesmerizing at the Book Fair. It was for the first time that she was visiting such a big Book Fair, especially with the heart and mind of an author. She decided to talk less and listen more so that she could understand the nuances of the industry. Her experiences and success as an Interior Designer would not mean much at this place. She knew that these few days were a learning opportunity for her and getting distracted would be wasteful. Her business mind told her to just be low key. People generally are more comfortable to talk openly in front of a dumb woman and she was ready to act like one. It was a calculated gamble that she decided to take.

Next day morning, they reached the venue again and she joined in a group of people who were keen to explore all the stalls. East, West, North, South and International were the 5 domes to be explored in 3 days. There were almost 250 to 300 kiosks, including stalls from publishers, authors, book stores, printing presses and creative designers. Some public relations consultants also did not miss the chance to be there.

'Let us all get divided in 5 groups and visit one dome each. That way we will be able to explore all 5 domes by evening. We will make notes about worth visiting stalls and exchange them at night. Next day the other group will visit only those stalls which are meaningful. This will not only save time, but we will also not miss out on any stall which is a must visit.' An (intelligent!!) man suggested (almost enforced). Most of them welcomed the idea and after some discussion they all started exploring the chosen dome with their respective groups.

'Worthy and meaningful to someone else could be worthless for me and vice versa,' Jiya thought for a while and decided to visit 'East India' dome. Kolkata – the name itself excited her with the thought of the richest literature of India. She smartly got involved with a group visiting that dome first. Jiya was hopeful to find something interesting there to start with. They walked through each stall for the first hour by the time Jiya realised that her taste and expectations varied from the group. She was really looking for something contemporary, while for others, East India meant Tagore and typical ancient Bengali flavor to look for. Jiya walked around with them listening to their conversations about how publishers operate and how to get on board with a decent publication house.

'If they all know so much about all this, then why have none of them actually published anything through any of these publishing houses?' She wondered and a sarcastic smile appeared on her face.

'What's so funny, Miss?' She was shaken out from her thoughts by a male voice.

Jiya snapped out of her thoughts and realised that she was holding a good-looking book in her hands, wearing a difficult to hide smile on face. She searched around for her mates who had left her behind to get caught by a random man with an odd smile on her face.

'Nothing at all. Please don't feel offended.' Jiya was slightly embarrassed realizing her smile was perceived as something offensive about the book she was holding.

'I saw a suppressed smile in your eyes. On a hot day, and under a hot dome, it can't be without a reason. You may tell me; I am here to receive genuine feedback for my book. I have written my heart out, wanting to touch some other hearts. So, tell me miss, what made you laugh about my book?'

'Hi, I am Jiya Juneja from Gujarat.' She offered her hand to the man, who looked at her curiously. Jiya's smile broadened.

'Ronit Basu, from Kolkata.' They shook hands. Ronit was a lanky guy, with mildly grown beard, not remarkably tall, fairer than usual East Indian men, with an appealing smile.

'Good to meet you and believe me, I did not mean to offend either your book or you. It was just a coincidence.' Saying so, Jiya ran to keep pace with her group. Her absence was not much noticed and neither did her joining back. 'One of the benefits of being silent and dumb' she thought and smiled again. Her suppressed smile was not at all noticed this time and she thought of Ronit who could read her eyes smiling louder than her lips.

'How did he know I was smiling?' Jiya remembered many people telling her that her eyes talked more than her words. Her smile did not leave her face and neither did Ronit's thoughts.

Over the dinner table, there was utter chaos, with 20 people exchanging information about the stalls worth visiting. Everyone wanted to prove themselves smarter than the others. It was not just loud, it seemed uncivilized too to Jiya. She missed her home, her parents, Sita and her comforting bedroom. She walked out of the dining area in search of fresh air and some peace.

'What a relief it is to be out here. I don't really know if it was the right decision to be here. I could have been sitting back home and making a better plan to explore the world of books, writers and publishers. This feels like a foolish hasty act. I wish Dad would have put down his foot and not allowed me to be here at all.' Jiya thought. She found herself an odd fit in the place, but she did not curse the place or people, for it after all it was her own decision to come here. She stood there for a while and made some plans to make the most of this visit on her own, instead of trying to fit into this group of people who were way different from her. She stood there a little longer, sipping the ice melting in her glass of water.

Next morning, Jiya woke up later than her roommate and waited for her roomie to leave to get ready. She had her own plans to visit all the publishers present there at the fair and meet a few of the PR consulting firms. She thought of it to be a smarter move than meeting authors and asking for their experiences.

Who knows if they would share genuine experiences or not? They will either want to show off that the publishing was a cakewalk as that their content was superb, or they will want the interviewer to believe that getting the book published was a challenge and it was a big achievement to get it published by a specific publishing house. Publishers will at least talk about their business and she would have genuine firsthand information, making her task easier. Acting dumb did not mean her business sense was dead.

She was walking through each stall of a publishing house and was all ears, picking up every word that was being spoken. By afternoon, she had met around 30 of them and was feeling good that she had been on her own, instead of following the list of worth visiting stalls according to some complete strangers. She had to move to another wing when she realised that her stomach was grumbling. She wanted to eat something local and decided to walk out of the venue. She walked in to a small joint suggested by some volunteers with plans to eat some soul filling and calories filled chaats and sweets.

While she was about to order, she saw Ronit sitting in the opposite joint, and she got out and walked into the place where he was.

'May I join you?' She asked courteously. Ronit could make out that it was a natural gesture and she was not faking.

'Oh sure, though I must tell you that I have not liked the food much over here.' Ronit said with a grumpy face.

'I know I can't have everything good at the same time. And right now, what I crave more for is a sensible conversation; and since I am starving, any food will taste good to me, Ronit. So may I?' She was still standing.

Rohit laughed, 'You are funny. Pull the chair please.' He pushed his plate towards Jiya, so that she could reach it. 'Come on, share my pain till the time you order some more for yourself.' Ronit played with words just like her and acted funny.

They ate some food from Ronit's plate while he started sharing his journey as a writer. While his experiences made her laugh, they also shocked Jiya at some places. Jiya also shared her background, her flaring practice as an interior designer and a little about her aspirations as a writer. She wanted to listen more, and reveal less.

'I want 'Bookworm Publication' to publish my book someday, but my pockets are not deep enough. Just the weight of my words does not support my intentions.' Ronit looked around trying to hide his tears.

'Keep writing, they will definitely accept your work one day. You don't need deep pockets all the time, sometimes depth of heart works just as fine.' Jiya could not relate with his frustration but felt something stirring within her for Ronit.

They walked back to the book fair. Ronit walked back to his stall and Jiya went ahead to explore the fair. A few hours later, she walked back to his stall with 2 cups of Coffee and some snacks. They chatted for a while, planning a dinner together the next day before they left for their respective cities.

While Jiya wore all high society swaggers on her sleeves, there was something about her that touched the middle classed Ronit. On the other hand Ronit's sleeve wore all the middle-class apprehensions, but the hidden spark inside him touched Jiya. They both realised that something was happening between them and it was likely to stay even after these 3 days of the book fair.

Jiya was dressed in her favorite little black dress paired with black bellies, and her usual makeup–a stroke of Kohl on her eyes and nude lip gloss. Ronit was dressed at his best, but Jiya looked way beyond his league.

'Jiya, I can't take you to Rivera, but I am sure you will enjoy this evening.' Ronit did not know if this was a formal date but the way Jiya was dressed, it felt like one. For a few initial moments, Ronit felt confused about how he should act around Jiya, but he then decided to be his natural self and the evening went well. Jiya found him different from other guys she had dated before. She realised how different financial backgrounds make a huge difference in personalities. She thought there was something very charming about him. They had a lovely dinner and Jiya laughed about the food they ate the last time together. They got comfortable telling more about themselves to each other. While Jiya opened up a little more than last time, she still chose to listen more instead of sharing much about herself.

'So, you will be leaving tomorrow morning, right?' Ronit asked as they strolled back to the ladies hostel where Jiya stayed with the other girls of the book club.

'Yes.' Jiya uttered a single word. She did not want to show her keenness to find ways of staying connected with him, which she wanted to.

'Jiya...' Ronit almost whispered. He couldn't understand all these measured words of Jiya.

Jiya stopped walking and looked at him. The whisper from Ronit was so powerful that it gave goose bumps to her.

'Yes, Ronit?'

'I would like to stay connected with you after we leave from here. I know the book fair organizers well and I can possibly sneak out your number from them, but I wouldn't do that ever. We will stay connected only if you wish to.' Ronit spoke his heart out and Jiya listened to him silently. She resumed walking and Ronit silently walked along her, silence raising the levels of his anxiety.

'2 3 X X 5 6 8 9 4 1' Jiya spoke her number leaving a space in between so that Ronit could remember it. She turned back, smiled and looked straight in to Ronit's eyes. Even before Ronit could smile back, she entered the hostel gate. He saved the number immediately.

He tried to hold himself but finally drafted a message on his cell phone. 'Thank you for sharing your number' and sent it to Jiya.

His cell phone beeped immediately. He had a big smile on his face and he did not to suppress it. He lifted his cell phone; the smile vanished and was replaced by a big frown.

'Message sending failed.' He couldn't think of any reason of this and felt extremely disappointed. He tried to think of various reasons for the failed message delivery– being out of balance, network issues, Jiya's phone being switched off. He once thought about calling to confirm the number, but dropped the idea considering the late hour. He decided to check the number with her next morning before she left. His could not sleep though, twisting and turning the whole night. As soon as the first rays of sun were visible, he quickly got ready and reached the dome of book fair, where all the visitors were expected to be found before departing. He waited for a while, and finding that Jiya did not turn up, his hopes were dashed. He decided to go to the hostel to see if he could find her there.

'They left ago an hour or so.' The watchman replied with disinterest. Ronit had to catch his train too. He knew that the journey back home meant long travelling hours. He would have loved the idea of being able to think about this beautiful and fierce girl for long hours during his train journey. However, at this moment, being clueless about what went wrong with the only source to be in touch with her made him loathe the long journey back home.

'Did she give a wrong number deliberately?' A thought hit his mind just to shoot up his anxiety. He couldn't resist going back to the book fair dome and meeting his friends from where he knew he could get her number. It was unplanned and he knew that this may risk his reaching the railway station on time, and even worse, missing the train, which would mean pounding from his boss and two unpaid leaves. But what mattered the most at this point was to get a hold of her number for two reasons; one – to get her correct number and two –to check if he made the mistake in saving the number or if she deliberately passed a wrong one to him.

In some time, he boarded the train with great peace again for two reasons; one – The legacy of Indian Railways continued with the train running behind schedule by 45 minutes. Two – he managed to have her number finally and would now be able to communicate to her.

He quickly settled on his seat and pulled out the piece of paper he had safe-guarded in his pocket carrying her number. 2 3 4 x x 6 8 9 1 4, he checked the number digit by digit and felt sad about doubting her for sharing a wrong number intentionally. 'Maybe, I messed a digit while I walked back to my room.' He couldn't hide the smile on his face. He missed Jiya badly. When his efforts to hide a smile failed, it invited a response from the uncle sitting on the opposite seat.

Chapter 3

‘Hi Jiya! ⊠‘He sent her a SMS. He counted seconds, minutes and hours until his phone beeped back.

‘Who is this?’ Jiya doubted it to be him.

Ronit’s heart sank for a moment over her reply, and soon recovered, consoling himself that she did not have his number so how was she to know that it was him!

‘Ronit Basu. Hope you remember.’ Sarcasm was difficult to hide there. He had not completely recovered from her cold response to his message which he had sent in great excitement. Then, Jiya was surprised by his reaction. She avoided writing anything immediately as she did not want the first digital conversation to start on a bitter note. She was aware about her own high self esteem, which could have really led the conversation to a bitter end.

Ronit expected her to continue the conversation but all he got was ‘wait’. His way back home was not as much fun as he had thought it would be; in fact, it was a total contrast. He travelled like an anxious and irritated man. 22 hours were filled with hurt, anxiety, pain, hopelessness and tempered ego.

Jiya decided to write to him after reaching back home and after resting in her own kingdom. She was missing

Sita's pampering, homemade food, conversations with her parents and her lavish bath. Before she could indulge in any of these things, her father welcomed her.

'Jiya, stop this drama of writing and all and if at all you can't do that, make sure you don't overrule me for it.' His voice was ice cold, but Jiya felt the fire beneath. She was looking forward to exchanging hugs and kisses with her parents but was shaken by this welcome. She stood there like a figurine, but her eyes struggled to hold her tears back. Once her dad walked away giving her a chilling gaze, she ran to her room. She locked her room and threw herself on the bed, sobbing. She tried to hide her sobs burying her face in the pillow. Sita and her Mom knocked on her door, but she said that she was heading for her shower.

'I will sleep after shower, please leave me alone for a while. I will see you people over dinner.' Jiya tried to be as soft as she could. She walked inside her bathroom, filled up the bathtub with warm water, added some of her favorite essential oils and soaked herself into it. Her phone was lying on the wash basin platform playing some music. She was really disturbed by the way her father had reacted over her decision. Music was not soothing her; she wanted to feel valued and get attended with care. The thought of Ronit hit her mind just then. The way he worked hard to get her correct number, pampered her ego and touched soft corners of her heart.

'How could I forget your sweet Bengali accent, deep eyes and intellectual conversation when I found myself a misfit in the environment that I was part of?' She wrote and smiled as she pressed the send button of her phone.

Beep… Ronit's phone beeped, and he picked it up immediately.

He loved the way the way the message was drafted, and his bitterness evaporated.

'If you couldn't forget any of these things then what took you so long to get in touch?' Complaints were still on the top of his mind.

'Now, when I already have, can we talk something worth a smile than getting stuck on whys and whats?'

Their chat continued. She felt well attended to and valued; she could sense that Ronit was fairly romantic, in addition to being sarcastic. They chatted for almost 3 hours and when Jiya got out of tub, she couldn't stop laughing over her wrinkled skin, making her look like an old woman.

Click.

'Is this what happens to a woman in a company of an interesting man?' she attached the photo of herself wrapped in a towel highlighting her wrinkled skin.

She applied lots of gel, wore some clothes that would help her hiding her wrinkles and save her from another encounter with her father. She was really under the impact of her long chat with Ronit. It really made her feel loved like never before, and she did not want anything else to hamper it.

'Lots of work is waiting for me, and I will have to face it all. I better stay off from the fury of a control freak man.' She loved her father but not his ego and intentions to be a ruler always.

Dinner began on a silent note. Silence was mysterious; she could not judge what was beneath it.

'I am sorry, Papa.' She said looking down at the plate, playing with her fork.

It was a big surprise for Tejas Juneja. He looked at her, he knew that his daughter was gifted with high ego genetically and didn't expect a sorry from her.

'Look at me Ginnie.' Jiya was relieved with that nick name being used, but still that chill in the voice was a sign of things not being normal.

She had no choice but to put the fork down and look at him. He winked and smiled and raised his wine glass at her.

'If you have done this to be with any guy, you need to know this before you get into any serious relationship. I will not approve of anyone who cannot afford your lifestyle, and this is non-negotiable.' The coldness in his voice gave more weight to his words.

'Papa, I was there just to explore a new passion, there is nothing to do about any man. I will not damage your fame and dignity ever, especially for any man.' She looked straight in his eyes and talked calmly. She was well trained by her father about how to be in control over emotions. Jiya's mind once again was hit by a thought of Ronit. She talked about her growing interest in writing to her father, and about her desire to get her book published.

'Do whatever you want wholeheartedly. Nothing should happen in a mediocre way. Also remember that as an author, it is your duty to give your best to your readers. You can buy everything else other than the sense of achievement. Even if you become a best-selling author using money, power and influence, you will know that it is not your victory and you would never be able to celebrate that victory from within.' Kinnary wondered if this man had all these morals hidden somewhere or was it just an attempt to be a hero in the eyes of his daughter.

She has been witnessing his hunger of winning by hook or by crook, but she still felt good seeing him teaching morals to their daughter.

Jiya finished her dinner quickly. Her phone was left for charging in her room and she was sure that by this time, Ronit would have messaged. She wanted to know his reaction on the photo she had sent and continue the chat with him.

'This is what happens when a very intelligent girl overlooks her smartness while being lost pampering herself in a bathtub.'

There were two more messages from him.

'And is this what happens to an average man, in the company of a good-looking, intellectual woman?' – A photo of a cut on cheek while shaving was attached along.

'I think you have again chosen to abandon your phone, and I would be expected to not ask what and why. I am resuming my work. Have a lovely evening.'

The gap between the two messages was around 25 minutes.

Jiya read his messages and realised that Ronit was annoyed with the long wait again. She zoomed in his picture with the cut cheek and saw it several times. She also tried to think if she really liked him and his company or was it just the need of an hour to overcome fatigue, need of attention, and need to fill up the absence of a man in her life. She could not decide anything, but could not resist drafting back a reply as well.

'Why don't you look at the other side of your persona? I am sure you would look better as a romantic hero than some medieval warrior fighting all the time.' She wanted to prove that she too was good at sarcasm.

As it beeped, Ronit lifted his phone immediately knowing very well that it was her. He read her message and disliked the fact that his discomforts felt funny to Jiya ever since they had headed back from Jaipur. Along with their own stories of discomforts, they still felt something special building between them, forcing them to overlook the discomforts and exploring more of each other. Their friendship quickly travelled from harmless flirting to sensual flirting.

'I wish someday I could use my fingers as pen and your body as a paper.' Ronit messaged her. Jiya was right in the middle of a discussion with a client about his new office. Jiya was a thorough professional and preferred not to use her cell phone for personal reasons while working. Quite a few things were changing lately, and this was one of them.

'Excuse me.' She almost rushed towards the restroom in her client's office, and it was not to answer the nature's call.

'I promise that it would be the best creation of yours.' She quickly typed back and turned the data off on her cell phone. She knew that keeping the internet on would drag her into a long conversation and she could not afford to do that now. She knew that she could connect with Ronit 24X7, but as a professional, to give her best to the client at that moment was the need of the hour.

She went back to the chamber and continued her discussion. She got free after an hour and half after her last text to Ronit. She knew that Ronit would have painted their conversation clipboard with some pessimism, but by this time she had learnt to handle it. She quickly turned the mobile data on and simultaneously she decided on the ways to conquer Ronit's reactions to such situation. She refreshed their conversations several times finding no reply from Ronit after her last text, which was unusual of him. She wondered if her last message had not been delivered to him for some technical reasons. After thinking for a while, she decided to resend her last message. She felt like appearing for an exam for a subject she had not prepared at all. Unlike his usual speed, she had to wait for a long time before she received his brief reply.

'Sure.'

'What's wrong Ronit?' She quickly typed back.

'Nothing at all. What made you think so?

'Why are you behaving so detached?'

'Not detached at all, I have just realised that it is a good time to learn to be calm when you are occupied with your work. I also think that I must learn to keep myself occupied with writing so that I can reach somewhere instead of waiting like a fool for you for hours.' He wasn't calm at all. This was the first time Jiya realised it how serious the situation was. She dialed his number. Most of the times, they communicated on chat apps on phones or by SMS during the day hours. Calling was not the regular mode to communicate.

Ronit too was surprised but had answered on the fifth ring and sounded very cold.

'Hi Ronit, what is bothering you? Me being busy?' She was straight to the point and very candid. Ronit had expected neither this call nor this question. He was clear that he was not ready being her option of entertainment. Spending hours chatting with her, only when she wanted was bothering him now.

'Not really Jiya, what makes you ask this?' Jia could not answer his question, but she felt that his sarcasm had been replaced by bitterness. She tried to gather words and cool down the situation.

'Nothing, I was missing you, so thought of calling you.' She was not confident if this would work.

'That's so nice of you, but I am busy with something now. Please excuse me. I will call you back once I get free.' He disconnected the phone and continued looking out of the window for a long time.

'What is the future of this relationship? She is out of my league. Would she even think of a future with someone who is middle class, who can't even afford one unpaid leave to be with her? I can't even dream of the cars that she uses. Where is the match? What is the purpose? Where do I stand in her life? Do I hold any significance in her life or am I just a tool for her entertainment that she starts flirting with whenever she wants?' Thoughts flooded him.

Same questions hit Jiya's mind too. What's the future? Am I ready for a serious relationship with him? If not, then why should I keep him hooked on to me? Is he just here to entertain me until I find someone worthy? Do I really feel something strong enough to forget the economic and cultural differences? She avoided facing those questions even though the answers had to come from her own self.

There remained silence between them for long. Both struggled with their hearts and minds, not to let their ego win.

Chapter 4

Jiya managed to patch up after some persuasion and they got back to talking terms. Sharing pictures, love notes, and everything was back to square one, but both knew that there was no future to all this, and they avoided talking about the same. There was a distinct coldness in some corner of their hearts, and every time Ronit touched that corner, he got bitter. Jiya got acquainted with his sarcasm and they learnt to find happiness between random uncalled sarcasm, bitterness and something that she couldn't name.

Jiya's love for writing did not subside along with her tight work schedule, or the time spent with Ronit. She was learning to craft her thoughts and emotions. She already had started dreaming herself as a successful author in the coming times. 'You are Tejas Juneja's daughter, nothing should be done in a mediocre manner.' Her father's words echoed in her mind. She often asked Ronit about the publication process he had followed during his first book but Ronit avoided answering the question.

'Ronit, please share your publishing experience, it would help me to avoid any mistakes which I might commit. I am ready with my manuscript and am very excited about publishing it. The only thing I need to work on is the publishing and marketing process.' She knew that Ronit will take his time to reply to her message. Jiya was fine with this new 'I am not available' approach. She knew that there was a huge difference in their professional and financial backgrounds; and it was bothering him seriously. She also knew that she was confused about what she wanted from this association with him.

'Madam, you have deep pockets and getting your book published through any good publishing house will not be as challenging as it is for someone like me. The story of my struggles will be of no help to you. My shallow pockets gave a hard time to me; you will not need to experience it. Everything is easy for rich people, especially when the person is an attractive woman. You have got everything that is needed to be a star.' He blurted almost everything that was stored within him for this long.

Jiya was taken aback and felt shattered for a while, but did not take very long to gather herself. She already knew that there was no future between them, but recent events were still disturbing. She had sensed insecurities, inferiority complex and growing jealousy in Ronit; which she was sure of being the reason to push them apart someday. All she did not think was that it would be serious disrespect and a thinly veiled attack on her character that would tear them apart. Jiya's self respect was hurt, and she would not allow anyone to do it. Things got messier following every event of her being busy, making Ronit feel as taken for granted. Waiting for her clueless, he got feelings of rejection and insult piling up inside of him. By every passing call, Ronit's words got nastier and Jiya started feeling more and more vulnerable; and today's eruption made it the worst.

'I am not a toy boy of a rich woman, who will be attended to only when she needs. If we are not lovers, we are not even acting just like friends too. I can't wait for you endlessly, while you finish everything else that matters more to you. You are rich and more occupied than me, but I too have things to do. I never make you wait for me and act pricey. I am not your toy boy who will entertain your ideas of romance whenever you want, Ms. Jiya Juneja.' Jiya hung up the phone, and the two of them never tried to talk again. They kept a very close watch on each other in every possible way though. Whatever the rationale was behind the spying, none of them compromised on their efforts to keep a watch on each other.

This unattended silence put ego of both on fire. They continued walking on the paths of achievements, not even knowing what exactly they wanted to achieve. Both focused on beating each other to prove their worth. One bond that could have possibly brought the best out of each happily was working the other way around. The sweetness, joy, possible love, possible togetherness, was all replaced by negativity, jealousy, and madness to prove oneself better than the other. It was neither war nor love, but everything was still considered fair. None of them knew that how far they would go, but both knew that there would be no limits on the opposite side.

Jiya's next year's plan was to be an author of a 'best seller', while Ronit started making his plans to get his next book published by one of the renowned publishing houses. He knew that it would not be as easy as it was for Jiya. Her success and her indifferent attitude towards him added fuel to his fire, making him more determined than ever to prove his mettle to her.

Jiya never forgot him completely; she was missing the way he made her feel good when things were better. She remembered the days when they talked for hours. Sometimes, she even felt like going back to him and to those old days, when they laughed and were soft and mushy towards each other. She always knew that Ronit belonged to a different culture and background. The pain he felt being hurt over petty issues was well known and experienced by her. Having said that, Jiya believed that whatever was building between them will change things soon. She could not take the fact that Ronit proved her wrong in a sadistic way. She wondered if she was really wrong? Was he wrong? Was the timing wrong? Was it the lack of future between them that was wrong? She wondered if there was love. She wondered if he was right stating that she used him for her own superficial romantic interests.

Ronit knew that his fight would be more challenging considering the facts that he would not be able to let go his job and focus on his writing, also that he was not as influential and rich as his opponent was. He chose not to use word 'enemy' for Jiya, even while he was introspecting.

Both continued their journey and walked on the paths of their choices to defeat their opponents. If it was not love, it was neither a war too. They were opponents for sure with the same motive – to win against each other. Jiya wanted to make sure to win it on her merits, but she left no stone unturned to make her first book brighter and shinier than Ronit's first. She exhausted all her resources to launch her first book. It was not a chartbuster yet, but it had started creating a buzz in the literary world. She knew this was way better than Ronit's first, and that was like winning the world war for her.

Ronit couldn't handle it. He tried to find peace behind the four walls. The days that followed came with depression, rage, bitterness and much more that detached Ronit from the world around him. This risked the chances of him finding relief spending time with any of his close ones. With heart filled of agony, he could not stop comparing himself with Jiya, her success, her achievements and her riches too. He could not avoid the bitterness building within him ever since her busy schedules made him feel not a priority in her life. He had liked her more than he had ever liked any other girl before, but the fact remained that she was out of his league. This realization did not let him settle. The coming days were challenging for Ronit, his family and his friends. They were all worried about Ronit trying to find peace in isolation, but there came a night when Ronit was seen sipping tea and watching TV like he usually did and laughing over some comedy show on TV.

Ronit found his peace in a decision that he made.

Jiya?

She was on cloud nine, she was absolutely enjoying her success. It was more of a victory than success for her. She had defeated her opponent, which was the prime reason of her joy, way above her first book making a mark. She was very sure that he followed her as much as she followed him secretly. Even if he did not, the bang of her achievement was loud enough to grab his attention.

'Congratulations, your riches bought the shining crown for you.' Though the message was received from an unknown number, she knew it was Ronit. She drafted multiple messages and deleted them, to draft a more bitter and harsher one. She felt extreme rage and wanted to give it back to Ronit. She could not understand what his problem was! She never had committed anything to Ronit, neither demanded it from him during their sweet, loving, mushy chats. Ronit too had never asked for any commitment directly or indirectly. What exactly troubled Ronit about her, remained an unanswered question that troubled her every day. She missed the sweetness they shared, but the bitterness was stronger. Combination of unattended questions, bitterness, pain, and frustration was lethal. She was now confused about her course of action; one message from Ronit ruined the charms of her success, or rather the victory.

Ultimately her wisdom convinced her not to reply at all. 'Ignoring it is the best solution'; she has been practicing this rule in her business, which she had learnt observing her father since childhood.

Getting dragged in non-productive arguments was not her way to fight the war.

She found her peace in a decision that she made.

Chapter 5

Canada.

This is where he knew he would make a lot of money to help him live his plans. The initial feelings of hurt, being ignored and being used made him boil with rage. It was definitely a war for Ronit now.

He was ready with a step by step plan and nothing could deviate him. His parents used all their emotional tools to stop him from leaving India, but failed. Leaving his parents, friends and his job behind, Ronit moved to Canada; a new world full of challenges made him even keener to fight and win. His struggles kept reminding him about the decision that he had made. He dealt with every struggle with power that he himself did not ever know he was loaded with. Conquering all those challenges boosted his confidence and he loved the feeling of this new grown confidence.

He found a decent job very soon, but kept his lifestyle restrained to save enough and for his plans. His parents continued surviving on their pension, but he did not send them much. He was learning the art of being ruthless and shrewd. Ronit came across some Indian businessmen, who needed his good command over English for their business purpose. He joined hands with them to make a few extra bucks. Time moved fast as if it was running a race with Ronit and his goals. Having collected a decent amount of money, Ronit was very sure now that it was his turn to execute his plans.

Jiya had moved on. She was very well aware that Ronit had moved to Canada and was settling down in a new world. She knew within her heart that he would not sit back silently, but the time passing in silence was confusing. He too would have moved on understanding his responsibilities, she liked to think. Jiya was a growing name in her designing profession too. Her success as an Author opened a new market for her and she was getting deeply engrossed in it. Hectic travelling schedule and writing aspirations kept her so busy that she was detaching herself from social engagements. She herself could not decide if she had got busier to stay away from the world or was she actually getting too busy resulting into distancing herself from the world!

'Beta, it is high time that we start looking for a life partner for you.' One morning Tejas Juneja shocked both the ladies on the breakfast table with one sentence.

'What is that, Papa?' Jiya reacted instantly. It was obvious that Tejas did not like the tone, but he was a very smart person. He looked straight in her eyes, and then at Kinnary. Kinnary's palm sweated; she knew the heat behind these cold eyes.

'Ginnie, I think you are growing too big and busy. Being a man, I know that no man would want his wife to be so busy so that she is rarely seen even on the breakfast table. Moreover, I think you are done with the chapter that inspired you to be a writer and do all that artistically fancy stuff.' Jiya was taken aback. It wasn't only Ronit who was spying; her dad too. She felt betrayed; her privacy was breached by her father. Soreness that had subsided just a while back was scratched again. This time it pained more than the last time around. At the end of the day, Ronit was no one to expect something from, but her father? The one whom she thought she was the most secured with had tried to peep in very personal areas of her life.

'Excuse me dad. I find this very intruding and insulting. I also want you to know that being a writer is my own aspiration and it will be forever. No one has ever inspired me to write and no one will ever be a reason for me to stop it.' Jiya's words were dipped in anger which shook Kinnary from within. Before she could do anything to cool Tejas, something unexpected and unprecedented happened—Tejas got up and slapped Jiya. Everyone was left baffled. Sita was almost on the verge of crying and left the scene immediately.

Jiya was stunned from within but she lifted her cup and continued sipping her tea, showing no interest to take her words back. She believed that her father had tried to peep into a part of her world which not only was unnecessary but was also much against her values.

'If you have someone on your mind, speak out right now. Once I will start looking for a good match for you, I will not consider your excuses. Get ready to get married, girl. This is what I have decided for you, and I see nothing intruding about a father wishing to get his daughter married to a deserving man.' Tejas said this very softly but both Kinnary and Jiya knew that there was a storm of anger behind.

No one talked to each other about the incident after that morning. Kinnary felt helpless but had no guts to talk to her daughter about what had happened. She knew that

Jiya was aware of her being a weak woman. She was so weak so that she did not stand up for even her own self respect or basic rights, and therefore there was no way she could lend help to Jiya!

After this incident Jiya got more determined to make strong marks in literary world. Her father was another reason in addition to the scars Ronit had given to her. Tejas Juneja triggered something strong, something very strong in Jiya. She was raging with a fire within that had the ability to burn everything around her.

'If money could buy everything; a toy boy wouldn't have dared to reject my riches Mister.' Long time had passed but she was still stuck in the moment; one reply was pending. Whether Ronit received that message or not, read it or not, she neither bothered to check nor did she wait for his reply.

The silence of her husband was bothering only Kinnary. Jiya was focused towards only one fact now that her next book must be a slap on the faces of everyone who challenged her credentials. She started completing every project under her interior designing firm at breakneck speed, so that she could get completely free from those commitments and attend to her passion.

She was working on a deadline to set herself free from the rat race of making money and creating fame, and all she wanted to do was to create something marvelous. She was so deeply involved in her work that she was hardly around at home. Her travelling became extensive and Kinnary perceived it as a sign of running away from her issues. She believed that Jiya avoided facing her parents after that stressed morning with her father. Kinnary was getting more and more confused about how to break her silence. She was not able to decide whether she should speak to Jiya or Tejas first. On one hand, her heart was supporting what Jiya was doing, on other hand her mind panicked seeing Jiya's determined actions. She felt terrified thinking about the efforts of breaking the silence with her husband; judging his moods was not her forte even after so many years of marriage. Silence suited her the most until turmoil hit the house.

She found her peace in a decision that she made.

While everyone was living in a comfortable silence, it was only Tejas who was restless. 'Being protective of my own daughter has made me feel like a culprit. She found me intruding for being careful about what company she was in. I have always behaved like a very close friend with her and have given much more freedom than other girls actually have. She is the one who hid facts about her romantic involvement with a boy and when I find it on my own, she finds me breaching her personal space.' These thoughts did not leave Tejas even for a minute.

'I was absolutely right in treating Kinnary in a high-handed manner. I think I made a mistake by giving liberty to Jiya. It was with my love and confidence that she learnt to live in dignity and grace. I was sure that I was her mentor and would forever be her guiding star, but she completely shattered my confidence and kicked my pride by stating I was intruding in her life. I cannot leave her alone to choose someone who is a complete misfit for a Juneja one more time.' These chains of thoughts dominated his sanity and he got all the more determined to take charge of Jiya's life. And he knew exactly how to do it!

He found his peace in the decision that he made.

Sita felt like the most ignored one after the event. Tejas would not want to face her, as slapping his own daughter in front of a maid made him feel small. Kinnary felt Sita's pain with the same intensity. She knew that facing Sita would mean facing the pain she must be carrying within. The knowledge that Sita must be living in a helpless state churned her soul every time she had to face her. Sita wondered that when a mother had no right to either stop or to oppose what has happened, what could she do? Ultimately, she was just the maid of the family. What hurt her most was that Jiya too avoided her after that morning. For all these years, Jiya would run to her and sleep in her lap even if she didn't talk about things that bothered her, but this time it was completely opposite.

She could not make any decision and found no peace.

Chapter 6

Canada.

Ronit was trying to look for a familiar face to kill time at the of wedding of Mr. Dixit's daughter. Mr. Dixit was one of his most lucrative business associates in Canada– Ronit looked after all his public communications. Dixit had started relying on Ronit's skills to communicate to clients and receive desired responses, which he always wanted, but could never make it happen until he met Ronit. Dixit was Ronit's favorite to work with. He was associated as consultant with many people in the literary word owing to his deep interest in literature.

'Why don't you work dedicatedly for me, I will pay you commensurately for that.' Dixit once offered him. By this time, Ronit had left his job as his freelancing associations brought stable money and offered him a lot of time to focus on his writing.

'I have some other aspirations which demand time and not just money, Sir.' He declined his proposal with grace. Every time Dixit paid him more than the deal, Ronit felt more respected and valued in Dixit's eyes.

Ronit was getting bored, hardly knowing anyone at that event. But he knew that leaving mid-way from there would look rude, and he could not afford to offend Dixit.

He started looking around to spot some company. There were a lot of Indian faces, few of them were Dixit's staff members whom he had crossed while visiting Dixit's office. Ronit felt uncomfortable with his shyness and the fact that he was always disinterested in meeting new people.

'If it is so, how come I became friends with her so soon and how come she came so close to me in the blink of an eye?' He was lost in the lanes of past, which felt soothing and troubling at the same time.

'Ronit, I want you to meet Nitya. She is our literary associate back in India. We work with her, but you may not know her by name as their work comes to us anonymously. I do trust you now enough for you to know some of such clients.' Ronit said hello and shook hands. Dixit excused him to attend other guests, leaving these two strangers alone in company of each other.

'I must say you are very good with your work, Ronit.' Nitya said with a smile.

'Doing my best makes me evolve, Madam, and some rare appraisals like this make me feel proud too.' He raised an eyebrow, while a small smile crossed his face.

'Nice to hear that. I work for Pigeon Publishing as their Creative Head. Mr. Dixit did not give you my detailed introduction.' Ronit shook her extended hand mildly with his sweaty palms. She looked at Ronit and saw some drops of sweat on his forehead. She couldn't stop laughing. Just after few seconds Ronit joined her too.

'What was that for? Me or Pigeon? Looks like Pigeon though.' Nitya asked.

'I am yet to decide but for now let's say a bit of both.' Nitya was a very good company. Ronit forgot the boredom he was facing at the wedding. In fact, he did not even realize the night was ending and that it was time to have dinner.

'You are a very good company, I must say.' There was a hesitation in his voice.

'You too.' She handed him her business card and left with a smile.

Ronit couldn't get that name out of his mind. 'Pigeon.' He got thinking, 'she gave her card to me, was it on purpose or mere business formality?' He was not able to judge but was tempted and excited to be close to her. Pigeon was his dream.

'Hi, am I talking to Miss Nitya?' Next day afternoon, Nitya answered a caller who sounded almost like he was whispering.

'Yes Ronit, you are talking to me.' Ronit heard a tinge of laughter in her words and found it embarrassing. What must she be thinking of me? She will certainly find me a desperate man who wants to speak to a beautiful woman who he was introduced to just a night before. He fumbled now, as his call was answered.

'Madam, umm…if you remember, we met last night.' He managed.

This one call was to change Ronit's life forever. It held the key that opened many locks in his life that was to come. He met Nitya several times over the next 10 days and found her very different than what he had thought she would be. It was a day before she was to leave for India, when Ronit felt his stomach churning. He didn't want her to go; he wanted her to stay and help him unlock some locks. Her leaving the next day would put him back to square one.

'Madam, you are leaving tomorrow, if you have some free time before that, I wanted to meet you for a while.' He called Nitya.

'Ronit, I have some tasks to finish before I leave. I won't be free before late evening. We can meet over dinner, if you know of any good place serving authentic Indian food.'

'I know of a fantastic place that serves food just like home. Let me know once you are free, Madam. I will pick you up for dinner.' Ronit's face was beaming.

He picked up Nitya and took her to his home. He had cooked some finger licking Bengali traditional food, which was certainly a tasty surprise for her. She profusely praised and thanked him for all the efforts he had put in and for being a wonderful and a warm host. They were standing in a small balcony holding their little plates of dessert.

'You wanted to meet me before I leave. I waited through the dinner for you to talk.' She was a professional and knew it well that he had a purpose behind all these.

Ronit was in a dilemma as to what should he say, or should he say anything at all? He chose to remain silent and tried to decide what is that he wanted to do now having been this close to this woman who could do something extraordinary for his future. The confusion was as to what, how and on top of all, why would she do anything for him!

Nitya gently put her hand on his. 'It is ok, you can tell me whatever is on your mind.'

Ronit had tears in his eyes before he started talking. They did not stop until he cried his heart out, talking about every single day from the day he met Jiya till the present day. He sat on the floor weeping. Nitya kept staring at him. Nitya decided to skip her flight for the next day and that turned out to be a ticket for Ronit to reach greater heights.

They both had several unanswered questions and that lifted Ronit's hopes of her handholding him on his path of reprisal.

'Nitya, will you please help me to regain all that I have left behind? Will you help me to put myself back into one piece? Will you please help me earn my pride back? Will you please walk with me while I walk on the road of reprisal?' Ronit knew that it was now or never; he had to ask whatever he wanted. His hopes were peaking because of the way things were shaping between them.

'Tell me what you want?' Nitya sat next to him on the floor noticing the fact that he addressed her as Nitya and not Madam anymore. They talked for a few more hours sitting there.

He found peace in a decision that he made.

'I will take tomorrow's flight back to India. Stay in touch on my personal number. We have got this close and that should be my reason to visit often. I will do the best that I can do for you.' She winked.

'Why don't you move to a bigger apartment? I will ask Mr. Dixit to find a better and bigger one for you, for us, rather.' Ronit nodded and blushed. He felt her taking charge of things, and quite liked it.

'Ronit, your new house is ready, you may shift today evening.' Dixit called him after a week. Ronit was baffled with the speed with which things started changing around him—a new home, a new car! He also stopped working with associates other than Mr. Dixit. Dixit started giving meaty assignments to Ronit and he was happy. Nitya visited him every month.

'Is everything set for you here, Ronit?' Nitya asked, playing with his hair.

'Absolutely yes.' Ronit wanted to know what she did about everything he had told her about Jiya and himself, but hesitated. She may feel that he was with her only because he wanted that favor, and he could not take the risk of losing her. She said that she would do her best, I should give her some time at least.

Ronit was so exhausted of pulling his cart on his own, that the moment he found support in Nitya, he willingly handed everything to her and clung upon her. He was also sure that Nitya was richer and more powerful to stand against Jiya, than he was alone.

One evening, he found Nitya's message on his answering machine to call back and he immediately did. He could not stop jumping out of excitement after hanging up the phone.

Chapter 7

Dear Ms. Jiya Juneja,

We covey our congratulations to you for making your first book a remarkable success. First time authors do not always receive such warm responses. Your efficient writing style and a strong plot has earned you what you deserved.

We are sure that books from our publication house would have touched your life too in the last 20 years. We believe in experimenting with new ideas in the literary world. We are planning to experiment with a co-author concept in near future. There is much more to this than the conventional approach of a book being written by two people together.

We are very sure that a young and progressive person like you would evaluate the concept with an open mind, and together we will be able to create something trendsetting.

If this idea interests you, consider this email as an invite to meet our Creative Head for further discussions.

Thanking you,

Team Pigeon Publishing House

* * *

Jiya noticed this email in her mailbox after three days from the date it was delivered. She swung between her heart filled with excitement, and mind struggling to hide the excitement. To be seen dancing in the office would not be as per the decorum she has maintained for years. 'It is Pigeon. Can you believe it Jiya, Pigeon? They want you to be part of something trendsetting.' She talked to herself.

'Seeing your secret smile after a very long time, Madam.' Zakir dared to say seeing that curling of lips she was trying so hard to hide but was visible through her eyes. Zakir had been working with Jiya ever since she did her first assignment as an interior designer. Zakir was a gift from Tejas Juneja to Jiya; he worked for Tejas before he was shifted to Jiya's office. He did not have any fixed work profile–he was her pantry boy, driver, mechanic, ticket agent, on site assistance and everything else that Jiya wanted him to be. Zakir knew Jiya enough to at least judge her moods and knew the way she liked her things to be done. He had witnessed her turning into a chirpy woman from a focused and serious businesswoman, and again being lost in her work in the recent past. The smile behind her eyes today was not hidden from Zakir.

He always admired her but also knew that she was too far away from his league. He was happy being a part of her journey to the best of his capacity. Driving her to nearby locations and dropping her home at no matter what time of the day, was the proof that he was the trusted one. He enjoyed the fact that it was he who was supposed to stay back with her in the office if she was working till late. Tejas Juneja would also have wanted Zakir to stay with her when she worked till late, so that he was sure that his Ginnie would be dropped back home safe.

Her recent phase of being behind the curtains was troubling Zakir, but he never had guts to ask her anything about it. The only brighter side of the change was she spent more time at work; she travelled more, meaning more time to spend around her for Zakir. He still missed the bubbly and chirping Jiya.

Seeing Jiya struggling to hide her smile made him happy, and he could not resist adding his observation. Jiya did not want to get caught smiling, but she already was. She stared at him, straight in his eyes. Zakir shivered a little and struggled to hide his awkwardness, wondering what that gaze was all about.

'Seems like you have laser eyes, Zakir! My smile is not visible on my face, but you managed to look behind my eyes.' Her broad smile was a feast for both of them.

'Come on, let's celebrate this smile. We are going to the Ahmedabad site. Get some food and sweets packed for the workers there. We will leave exactly after an hour.' Zakir could not even judge if it was all for real. He left the place immediately lest Jiya changed her mind.

'I will be late; I am going to the Ahmedabad site. Zakir is driving me and he will drop me back home too.' Jiya sent this message to all the three people who should be updated about her whereabouts – Tejas, Kinnary and Sita. Completing this project would mean that she would get over all her major assignments and would soon be free to focus on the decision she has made.

Zakir was driving at the speed suiting her comforts, one of her favorite music tracks was playing, and she was munching her favorite snack. Something unusual was happening though. Her phone was silent; she was calmer than her usual anxious state of mind. She suddenly asked Zakir to stop the car, got off from the rear seat and sat on the front seat. She took off her shoes, turned around, folded her legs, rested the back of her head on the dashboard and started staring at the roof of the car.

'Speed up Zakir, we must reach there as soon as possible. We have a lot of work to be finished, and I have no plans to stay back. Also please turn the music off.' Zakir raised his eyebrows and looked at her.

'You find me behaving strangely today, isn't it?' She laughed as she said this. Zakir was perplexed; she had never behaved or talked to him like this.

'Zakir, have you ever loved someone? Jiya asked him. He looked at her; her eyes were closed and had prominent frown lines on her forehead.

'Ma'am, *pyaar to sabhi karte he na..*' (Everyone loves someone or the other.)

'How difficult does life becomes when you do not really know if you love someone or not, and even before you realize anything, misunderstandings create a wall of bitterness between the two.' Jiya was not bothered if Zakir could even listen to her while she uttered all these words.

Zakir could not understand her, but all he could make out was that she was trying to come to terms with something which was bothering her for long. Maybe the reason behind the hidden smile was encouraging her to get rid of all these issues. She wanted to look at new things coming to her under a bright light, away from the darkness of the past. Zakir said nothing and continued driving. He looked at her after a while, and saw tears rolling down her eyes. Zakir had seen her getting angry and shouting, getting anxious and shouting, getting overjoyed and shouting, getting under the deadline pressures and shouting, resting and shouting over getting disturbed, and shouting over almost everything that happened around her but never had seen her being this silent and crying.

'Shall we stop by somewhere for a cup of tea, ma'am?' Zakir tried to distract her.

'No, and please speed up.'

Zakir followed the instructions. As the car sped up, so did the flow of her tears! Zakir stopped the car.

'Why have you stopped?' Jiya asked without opening her eyes. Her head was still rested on the dashboard; Zakir could see her without even turning his face towards her. She looked tired and lost; she didn't want to stop the chain of her thoughts which were faster than the speed of the car.

'Jiya, we have reached.' Zakir wanted to take his words back. He knew that addressing her with her first name could mean losing his job. Perhaps she did not even notice him using her first name. She opened her eyes, turned around and sat properly, looked at herself in the vanity mirror, and laughed aloud. Her Kohl had spread all around her eyes, and the traces of tears merged with it, had left stains on her cheeks. She could not stop laughing, and Zakir knew exactly what she was trying to do. Jiya tried to hide her tears behind her laughter. She pulled out a face wipe to clean her face and approached her work.

Zakir handed over the food and sweets brought along to her and said, 'We have a reason to celebrate, and we need to smile when we celebrate. Isn't it?' He had a broad smile and Jiya smiled back.

'Let's celebrate!' She said with a beaming face, grabbing all the bags from Zakir's hand. She almost ran in the direction of the site where all the workers were waiting for her. Zakir waited for her inside the car. He smoked more than his usual, as he was constantly thinking about what he witnessed during their drive. He stood clueless about the changes in Jiya.

The Sun had started setting, Zakir called on Jiya's phone which remained unanswered. He knew that he had to wait; an hour later Jiya knocked on the glass of the car, Zakir woke up and realised he was sleeping. It was already 11 in the night.

'Let's go. I will drive you back. You please sleep and relax. I am really sorry for the delay.' Jiya was fresh and completely opposite of what she was while coming. Jiya was adamant over the idea of her driving back home. Zakir surrendered after a few minutes of arguments. Jiya was driving him back, and he could not stop laughing. He laughed and Jiya joined in too. Both had different reasons to laugh, but it did not matter to either of them.

'Ma'am, I am not sure about love, but I liked someone very much.' Zakir said blushing just after the moments of laughter.

'Zakir, forget about whatever happened on our way to Ahmedabad. Forget about the questions asked, statements made, tears rolled, bury all of them this very moment.' Saying this Jiya did something very unexpected; she handed 5 notes of 500 Rupees to him. Zakir did not touch them and continued looking out of window. She pulled her hand back and turned her eyes back on the road. Her face was expressionless.

Just when they were about to reach home, Zakir said, 'Ma'am, maybe everything that is on sale can be bought, but it is not necessary that everything is on sell.' This time, he looked straight into Jiya's eyes.

Chapter 8

Jiya had learnt to wait not just during her professional practices, but by observing her father too. Being too desperate was the sign of weakness, and that would not keep you one up in the deal. She took her time to reply to Pigeon, but this email had triggered many emotions inside of her.

It made her feel so proud of herself that she was the chosen one and at the same time remembering Ronit's last words choked her. She was not able to digest the fact that Ronit found her achievements so despicable. If they were not in love, they were not enemies either. She lost her self-control in front of Zakir under the impact of the vacuum Ronit had created, and it was an alarming situation. Being seen as a weak person was not acceptable to the Junejas at all. But Zakir's words and his changed behavior threw her back in state of guilt. She was confused if she used her riches and power to win or was she really potent enough to stand where she was standing today? She was thrown back to old times when she had to make a major decision about her further studies.

'Ginnie, why don't you agree to go to a foreign country? Many students have no choice but to settle down for any domestic institute following their financial limitations, but you are Jiya Juneja—Jiya Tejas Juneja. Pick up the best university, if you don't get in on merit, we will go for the payment seat.' Tejas wanted the best for her and was sure that with the money and power that he held, he could buy anything he wanted for her daughter.

'Let her study where she gets in according to her merits. She might get the best education on payment seat, but she will learn a wrong lesson for life.' Kinnary opined.

Tejas looked at her with fury in his eyes. It was a clear message for Kinnary that she must remain silent. She understood and left the discussion instantly. She was hurt and failed to hold back her tears from flowing as she reached the safest corner to cry – her kitchen. In the eyes of Tejas, the kitchen was a corner for ladies and maids and he hardly entered there. Sita rested her hand on Kinnary's shoulder; she turned around and hugged Sita, this had happened for the first time.

'Why can't I teach some of my values to my own daughter, Sita?' Kinnary murmured as she wept.

'Papa, I know you want me to have the best. But my dearest papa, experience is the best school. My grandfather always said, 'win the world with your merits and hard work'. I don't want anybody to point at my achievements as a product of my father's riches and supremacy. Please understand my thoughts and feelings.' In the other room, Jiya was shivering because of either fear of her father or fire within to win the world.

'Jiya, I don't want you to repent later. Degree from the best of the colleges will fetch you finest clients. Your decision to the contrary will mean that you will not be able to use my network in future.' Tejas continued to look away while saying such vicious words.

'Please look at me, Papa. Do you really want me to be known only as the daughter of Mr. Tejas Juneja forever? Would you not be happy if I build my own fame and create my own legacy? I am not ready to believe that your ego can dominate your love so much that you would not let your daughter spread her wings.' Jiya won the battle the moment she saw a tear rolling down his eyes.

'Go and live your dream. I am carrying the legacy of Junejas since years but could never be known as Tejas. Go and be Jiya. I have faith in you that while building your fame, you will not commit a mistake that will defame the Junejas legacy. While it certainly is difficult to earn fame, it is very difficult to maintain a legacy.' They hugged and Jiya enrolled herself to the best available choice to persuade her degree on her merits in India.

Kinnary and Sita were finally happy; Kinnary chose to look at the brighter side overlooking her motherhood being ignored. She was happy that her daughter made the right choice, and she was not dominated by her father, which was the happiest part of the incident.

The incident played like a flashback in her mind. She was smiling and looked around to make sure no one observed her getting emotional. She was even more determined to rub the traces of the past and live the present that was knocking on her door.

'Jiya, you are definitely good but not the best. Business practices are not the standard way to deal with everything. You must write back to Pigeon without wasting time. You are definitely not the only one they would have sent that email to.' She thought. She was ready to reply to Pigeon immediately. She was sure that this would be the most appropriate way to slap the faces that claimed her achievements were result of her riches and famous legacy of the Junejas.

'I will not lose this; Junejas never lose anything they want to win.' She thought aloud.

She was worried that it was too late to reply, and someone else might have got on board. She could not decide if she was foolish or smart by delaying sending her reply. She turned on her laptop; restlessness towered over her mind until her mailbox opened. Keeping them crossed for long, her fingers pained.

Respected Team Pigeon,

I extend my heartfelt gratitude for your wishes on my success. I take this opportunity to thank you for publishing such high-quality literature to benefit readers of each age group and social background for the last so many years. Publishing houses like yours not only motivate the writers like us to work harder, but also the readers to read quality literature.

I am not only overjoyed, but pleasantly surprised on receiving your offer. Co-authoring is an idea that has always excited me. I am looking forward to knowing more about the proposal. I am determined to give my best to my next book. I am sure that under the guidance of team Pigeon, I will be able to do wonders.

I would love to meet your Creative Head at the earliest mutual convenience and get the process rolling.

With gratitude,

Sincerely,

Jiya Juneja.

All she knew was that she had to wait. She also knew that this wait could be sheer 'wait' that could result into nothing. Maybe the selection of co-authors is already made. She thought of crossing the fingers once again, but the pain she experienced just a while back pushed her to drop the idea. She was desperately waiting for that one ping in her mailbox. She found herself waiting for something this desperate after a long time.

A chain of incidents and emotions started occupying her mind again. She remembered her early days of communication with Ronit with no intention of committing herself to him. She loved the fact that Ronit was attracted towards her so much that he managed to find her number, even though it meant risking missing his train and taking obligations from the Book Fair Organizers. With passing time their friendship grew. Jiya was hooked by Ronit's idea of romance and the fact that he had so much prowess in expressing his affection. She could not stop him from establishing a bond between them which she never was ready for.

Jiya wondered now if she had ever loved him? She remembered how she waited for his messages, calls and emails. No electronic medium of communication remained unused by them. Ronit's promptness to reply to her each message gave her a feeling of being wanted. She would check her phone even during her client meetings to read his sugar loaded words even if she could not reply. It was very rare that she used her phone during work before Ronit happened to her. His sarcasm about she being ignorant and rude made her feel his desperation, but she loved the fact that he craved for her. She secretly knew that she craved for him as much as he did, or else Jiya Juneja who made people around her to wait for her, would not wait for someone like this.

She sighed, 'I wish I would have known that his unattended desperation would turn his sarcasm into bitterness.'

She opened her mailbox to check if she received any reply.

She sighed again. Why would they reply to me instantly? It has just been a few hours that I have replied to their email. I must learn to wait, not everyone is Ronit, who is sitting holding phone in his hand to reply to me all the time. She disliked the way she dominated their relationship and found her solely responsible for the reason why things went wrong between them.

Shall I start working upon my book independently? Shall I wait for Pigeon to revert? Shall I pick up an interior designing assignment in between to stay occupied? My idle mind will keep troubling me and will bring back memories which I really want to go away from. Ronit seems to have moved on and I must too. Life in Canada will bring glory and hopefully more success, helping him overcome his inferiority complex. She was lured to check his facebook profile and find out how he was doing. She was disappointed to find that his profile was not updated after he had left the country. Maybe Ronit had blocked her to stop her from stalking him. I am a wicked woman, am I not? Be it my mother, Sita, my dad, Ronit or even Zakir, I have manipulated them to suit my comforts, if not for my benefits. After the last incident with papa, mom and Sita must have wanted to talk to me and console me. But I have been neglecting them because I was not, and I still am not comfortable to talk to either of them. I broke the walls of distance with Zakir, just because I wanted to give a vent to everything clogged inside of me. It was I who asked the question to him about love, and signaled friendship, and by the time he gathered his guts to answer, I pulled myself back. She looked at the vacant corner Zakir occupied till few days before, and now he had cornered himself just to stay away from her.

Ronit's words echoed in her mind and heart again.

'I am not your toy boy, who will entertain your romantic needs only whenever you want Ms. Jiya Juneja.' She felt a rush of disgust for herself. How self-centered and materialistic I have become that I cannot respect other person's state of mind or heart. I have become a replica of my father. Every time he insulted or mistreated her mother just to establish his powers and superiority, she promised herself that she will never follow suit. Tears started rolling and she found herself choking, full of emotions. She wanted to run away from everything, everyone, even herself.

'Using people for personal interest and to leave them stranded once your job is done is the worst one can do.' Kinnary had once told her; tears again started rolling down.

Jiya picked up her bag and left the office, she seeked some fresh air to get her thoughts straight. She settled down in the back seat and Zakir got the car moving.

'Take the car on highway and don't stop. Turn the AC on and the music off.' Jiya pulled on her glares and rested her head on the head rest of her luxurious car. She was weeping with closed eyes. After an hour or two, Zakir felt confused about how long he should keep driving, they were far away from the city by then. Jiya's chilling silence and occasional sobs troubled him. He looked at her in the rear-view mirror.

'Drop me home, Zakir.'

'I am sorry for the other day.' She said just these two sentences in last couple of minutes, to which Zakir responded with no words.

'Don't be sorry, Madam, I know the pain of heartbreak.' Zakir looked at her in the rear-view mirror.

'It's not heart break.' She wanted to make it clear to him that no walls were broken around her. The car slowed to stop in the porch of her home. She hadn't realized how long she had been out but it seemed like minutes. The pain hadn't subsided. And she knew it would not soon.

She rushed to her mother's room and broke into tears on her bed. Kinnary hugged her and called out loud for Sita. Sita rushed to her room and did not take much to understand that Jiya was tired of storing unattended feelings inside. Sita had observed her growing as a chirpy and a happy person; she was also observing all that life vanishing off one by one, leaving Jiya restless and lost. Sita started caressing Jiya's back slowly and let her give vent to everything that was bothering her without asking a question.

Jiya heard a ping on her phone. She sat up to check it (she just wanted to avoid questions, and cell phone was the immediate excuse available) Her cell phone changed her mood like London's weather. She was jumping and dancing on the bed and passed hugs and kisses to the ladies in the room. She called up her dad to share the news.

'I am invited to meet the Creative Head of Pigeon Publishing, papa! It is time to create my own legacy. I will add more to the Junejas' glory, papa.' She looked at the two ladies and they were smiling with surprise written all over their faces, not really knowing what was happening.

* * *

Jiya was sitting in front of Nitya. The two of them had traits to impress each other. Jiya thought that with the creative mind that Nitya had, which also understood business efficiently, she was a good fit for the position of 'Creative Head' of such a well-known publishing house. Jiya was enamored by how Nitya evaluated business and how sorted she was. She wondered as to whether she was handling her own business this efficiently. Nitya was a woman of few words; she listened more and talked less. But whatever she said was enough for Jiya to understand what was on the cards.

While Jiya was getting charmed by Nitya, Nitya was finding Jiya's achievements pretty striking. 'At this young age, she is making her own mark. Belonging to a family with royal legacies, she has independent aspirations, which showcases her independent and self-relied persona.' Nitya thought about the bequest of Junejas' and that made her look at this girl under very bright light. She had designed the idea and explained almost all of it to Jiya, to which Jiya agreed without too many questions.

'Jiya, I believe that you agree with the structure and terms of the project.' Nitya was looking forward to freezing an agreement with Jiya.

'I agree with the terms, in fact I am quite positive about the way you have designed this, Nitya. Something makes me curious about the whole thing and this excites me even more to be a part of it. I have a few queries, if you don't mind.' Jiya was a woman with brains and she would never jump into anything without digging more about it.

'Feel free to ask and discuss. I want you to be part of it will full conviction.' Nitya got up from her chair and sat on the one very next to Jiya.

'I think knowing my co-author will let me create a better understanding about him or her and we will be able to create something more powerful. Having a stranger on the other side is likely to create some discomfort and distance.' Jiya really wanted to know about the other half–the other part of the story.

'Jiya it really took us long to design this experiment. Two known people, sharing the same wavelength, with the same understanding on a subject is a very much explored way of co-authoring. We do not want any personal interactions between the two authors of this book. If you are not comfortable and want to rethink, you may take a week's time.' Nitya was sure about this question coming and she was well prepared to address it.

'Jiya, you are certainly our first choice to do this, but we are already delayed with our plans due to your delayed reply. We cannot wait for more than a week. You will be given an official email id, which will be the only medium to communicate with your counterpart until the final manuscript is handed to us.'

Jiya took a pause, smiled and said, 'Please get the contract printed, let us do it now.'

Jiya spent a little more time with Nitya in her chamber while they finished the formalities and left with a big smile on her face. She observed a man with a good physique, style and an arrogant walk enter the Pigeon house. He got closer and exchanged a smile with her, and that smile made her skip a heartbeat.

It was Ronit.

With his smile, he tried to hide all the bitterness he held. He wanted her to believe that he was not shocked or surprised to see her. Little can be said if he succeeded in his effort or not, but Jiya was definitely perplexed and she did not try to hide that at all.

'Hi, how come you are here?' She was straight to the point.

'Still the same, Miss. Jiya Juneja. What makes you think that I cannot be here?' It did not take a fraction of a second for Ronit to answer.

'Still the same, Mr. Ronit Basu. What made you think I meant only what you think I did?' Jiya was irritated to find him still as sarcastic as ever. Maybe, even worse. His visual transformation had given some hope to her of him having sobered down. Sadly, it wasn't so. He smiled at her and walked away. She saw him entering Nitya's cabin without even knocking on the door. This was really overwhelming for Jiya. She looked in his direction for a short while before she walked out of the fancy building.

'What is he doing here? Shall I directly ask Nitya about him? Could he be my Co-Author? Could life be really filled with such coincidences?' Her head flooded with a lot of questions as she tried to find the answers. She was so lost in her thoughts that she almost banged her head on the glass door.

Chapter 9

Canada.

The alarm continued to blare until he snoozed it. It was 5 a.m. and like many others, Ronit was about to kick start his day. It rang one more time and Ronit threw away his blanket and jumped out of the bed. He put his toothbrush in his mouth and started brewing his coffee. He pulled out a bread box, pulled out two slices and buttered them, still holding the brush in his mouth. Suddenly he remembered something, threw everything aside and rushed towards the bathroom. He quickly brushed his teeth, gargled and had a quick shower. He got out of the bathroom in his blue bathrobe, rushed to the kitchen, gulped down the coffee that was not hot anymore, with slices of the bread and ran towards the dressing area. He knew what he was supposed to wear. He thought he looked perfect in his white shirt and grey jeans. He smiled, and not being sure of her reaction on seeing him, left the house with his car keys.

Ronit loved his newly built up body. It had been a long time here in Canada and a lot of things had changed about him and in his life. 'I am no more a dependent on my parents' pensions and my negligible salary. I am no more the boy next door, who would wear the same jeans for 3 days and change it to the only other pair he possessed. I am no more a man who waits for his woman to contact him all day long just because he knows that he holds nothing to attract her. I am no more a man who would not dream to date a rich woman just because he cannot afford to date her. I have learned to carry branded fashion and have also learned how to earn enough to buy them as well. I have worked hard to develop this desirable body to carry all these brands well that I can really model for some of them. I have mastered all those charms and have earned enough to impress any girl and can date her as long as I want.' After thinking of all these things, something churned his heart. He remembered the time when he had first meet Jiya. Eating distasteful food in a dingy food joint on the streets of Jaipur still felt the most innocent and the most desired moments of his life. The chain of his thoughts broke as his cell phone rang.

'25 minutes.' She said.

'Sure, I won't be late, I am already on my way.' He said with a fake smile which could be the result of the disturbance on the thoughts of his glorious past.

She hung up. He wondered how long she would stay back but pushed him to focus on what her arrival would bring in his life. He did not want anything to let him deviate from his goal.

'What was so glorious about that past that you still miss those days, Ronit? You had no money, your own parents did not find you worthy, you wrote one book which could do no wonders, you ran after a girl who was much more successful than you, and you acted foolishly by letting her use you at her convenience.

Focus on what you have managed to do today–a decent house, handsome bank balance, happy parents who feel proud of you, the way you look, the number of fan following that you have, including a lot of female fans, and on top of it, you will soon have a book which will be a super hit, making all your dreams come true.' He reached the airport within the given 25 minutes, lost in thoughts of his past, present, and future while driving mechanically.

He checked the time on his watch, which brought a big smile on his face. He had managed to reach the airport before time, but the smile was there because of the brand of watch on his wrist, the name of which he could not even pronounce back in India. He saw her coming from a distance and a lump of saliva rolled down his throat, reminding him that his throat was drying up with each step that she took towards him. Feeling of discomfort passed through his spine, thinking of her being there for next few days. He quickly opened his email box, checked her last email which made him feel good and remain focused about what all he needed to do further. As soon as she was 100 steps away, he jumped out of the car, ran towards her and reached out to her.

'Hey gorgeous, it's so good to see you.' he said hugging her.

'Let's run home.' She said with a smile. She did not look tired or stressed even after this long a journey. Her makeup was still intact, her dress uncrumpled, and she looked as fresh as if she had just walked out of a salon. He took over her luggage trolley and she started walking alongside him holding him by his bicep.

Though Nitya looked elder than Ronit, she was charming enough to compliment him. With a good height, fair complexion, a reasonably toned body and a good sense of fashion, she looked classy. The confidence in her body language was a sure sign that she was either born rich or was a powerful businesswoman.

Nitya occupied the driver's seat and Ronit knew that she would not let him drive for all the days she was there. He fastened his seat belt and they zoomed away from the airport.

'I was desperately waiting for this moment.' She said looking at him.

'I did not know that this car and these roads are so precious to you.' He said winking at her.

She sped a little more and in the next 7 minutes, she parked her car in a parking zone and almost jumped on him.

'This–you stupid, this. I couldn't wait for you. For being just next to you, for being just by your side, for doing all the things that we will do all these days.' They kissed for a long time and talked about how much they longed for this togetherness.

'Will you be able to handle the steering now, or shall I?' Even before Ronit could complete his question she accelerated, the car sped at the speed of 120 mph and was booming with each passing second. Ronit started worrying with the increasing speed of the car but could not do much. He felt a great relief as they reached home.

'Thank God, I am no more at the risk of dying on the roads of Canada.' He smirked.

'That does not assure you that you won't be dying at all.' She winked and he continued smiling at her. She threw away everything in her hands and dragged him to bed. She had waited for him for so long and was determined to live every minute and moment she had let go of all these days. He too was determined to make her live everything that she would have missed. They went out for dinner with the faces that looked happy but tired; the passersby and restaurant staff could not hide their smiles looking at the love bites – obvious reason of fatigue on their faces.

'You order food, Ronit, I will choose wine.' Nitya was wearing a black Jeans paired with a neon green T-back top. Painted toes peeping through her flip flops were a clear proof of how meticulously she carried herself all the time. Every time she smiled, the wrinkles around her eyes and lips got prominent. She did not even try to hide her wrinkles, which was a sign of her high self-confidence.

Ronit stared at her. She was flawless. There was not a single thing that he could point out that suggested a scope of improvement. Was there anything that was not likeable about her? She was powerful, brainy, had a body to die for, successful, jolly, classy and rich too. She must have made lots of men envious of Ronit for having her by his side and women too for not being able to be like her. These were the traits that made her unmatchable. She loved being like this – confident, rich, successful and powerful. All she wanted to live was riches; she believed that rest will follow by hook or by crook.

She ordered a Chardonnay and Ronit ordered her favorite pasta, followed by some light starters to make her happy. They were very hungry after burning that lot of calories, which made them hog everything that came in front of them. Nitya ordered one more bottle of wine, which confirmed Ronit's premonition that they were not going back home that night.

'Ronit, let's not go home tonight. I want you to have the best of me right now.' Her words spluttered, but not her intentions. Ronit was all prepared to have a long night followed by a brighter morning.

'As you wish, I will go and get the room booked, please excuse me for a while. You may sip more of that red passion till then.' He walked towards the reception area of the hotel.

'How may I help you, Sir?' the person at the reception kept on repeating this multiple time until the chain of his thoughts was broken.

He was shaken a little when he was addressed a little loudly. He found himself standing there at the reception, lost in thoughts. The person at the reception was confused and the lady sitting on the travel desk nearby was getting irritated following the chaos around.

'How may I help you?' Ronit did not like being addressed loudly, but he did not react at it, knowing that it was a reaction to his dumb behavior at the reception counter.

'I need a room for a night, preferably a suite.' He knew her taste and did not want to compromise on anything. Her happiness meant the world to him, and only he knew the reasons.

'Sure, Sir. By which name shall I book the room?' This guy asked with an artificially sweet formal voice. Ronit loathed this sweetness; he found everything fake around and sighed. 'Ronit Basu', he said pulling out a small pile of dollars and placed along with his identity card to follow the formalities. The formalities once done, they went to their room.

Ronit was determined to make Nitya happy and Nitya was determined to live her happiness. They woke up with smiles on their faces next morning. Nitya loved the way Ronit filled her and made her feel. She could not have asked for more.

Over the breakfast table, with the subsided hangover of alcohol, but not Ronit's for Nitya; she shared some business plans with him. He was very sure that he was not supposed to give any suggestions, but just listen and admire them. He had learnt to pamper her ego and make her happy. She showed some of her recent photos to him, to which he offered some kisses and whispered some romantic words in her ears, making her blush.

He sensed it to be the right time to show her an email on his cell phone.

'I am sure you would have seen this email. I cannot wait for this going ahead now. Thank you so much for everything.'

They looked at each other and kissed passionately for a long time.

Dear Mr. Ronit,

We want to congratulate you for penning a remarkable book. First time authors do not always receive such warm response from readers, but that should not be the only parameter to judge the quality and efforts of the creation. Our creative team appreciates your writing skills.

We are sure that books published from our publication house would have touched your life over the last 20 years.

We are a publishing house which believes in experimenting with new ideas in the literary world. We wish to experiment the co-authoring concept in line with our approach.

We are sure that a young and progressive mind like you would evaluate the concept with an open mind, and together we will be able to create something that is trendsetting.

If the idea interests you, we would like to invite you to meet our Creative Head for further discussion.

Thanking you,

Team Pigeon Publishing house

She gazed deep in his eyes for a long time, making him uncomfortable.

'Do you really want to do this, Ronit?' Her voice shook a bit. She sounded worried about Ronit getting into this.

'Absolutely Yes, Nitya. I cannot let this go at all, not at this stage. Not at any cost.' This time Nitya heard something very strong, something like a storm building behind his words.

Rohit feared what if this lady stepped back on her words. He has compromised on many things which he never thought in life he would do. He could not afford to let Nitya think other than what was decided.

'Oh absolutely, you gonna do it.' She uttered while being lost in thoughts of what future was holding for each of them.

Chapter 10

Time takes a real test of powerful people. One may buy everything he wants and may dominate the world, but what one cannot buy or dominate is 'Time'. Jiya Juneja knew it very well. The pain that she had carried inside of her had subsided quite a bit after pouring her heart out to her mother and Sita.

'Papa, I am sorry for whatever has happened lately between us.' Sita stopped on her way back to the kitchen hearing this, Tejas kept his coffee mug back on the table silently and Kinnary stopped eating and looked at Tejas instantly.

'Relax guys! Sita Mata, please go ahead and get his toasts; he does not like them cold. I want you to be here once you bring them. I want to say something to all three of you.'

All three of them were baffled, since silence was the norm in the house ever since Tejas had slapped Jiya. Sita almost ran inside the kitchen, quickly grabbed 2 toasts and dumped them on Tejas's plate. She completely forgot to butter them and Tejas ignored that error with grace. All three of them were all ears to what Jiya was about to say.

The first thing they heard was Jiya's laughter. They failed to understand what was happening, but all three of them looked at each other and smiled. Jiya's smile was a rare sight these days; her genuine laughter was like a bonus for them. Sita and Kinnary did not try to hide their tears after they saw Tejas letting them flow. Jiya ran to him and they hugged, Jiya asked Kinnary too to join the embrace. Kinnary could not recall when she had been this close to Tejas in the near past. Sita too let her tears flow, she was happy to see this reunion. She cleared her throat, trying to attract their attention.

'I think I shall come in the evening to listen to what you wanted to share, Jiya,' she acted funny. They all laughed together.

'I cannot make you wait, Sita Mata, especially now when I know how much it hurts to wait. I want to say sorry for my detachment, my harsh words, and everything that I have been hiding from all of you all these days. You are my parents, and Sita too has raised me and is just like a mother to me. I have introspected enough to realize why I hurt Papa so much so that he had to slap me. I think I should share this with you all, that I had a guy in my life.'

Kinnary interrupted 'Do you love him, beta?'

'I intend telling you everything, and I hope you will believe in every word I say. I did not love him, neither did he. However, we were close, and we shared a very good romantic wavelength. We used to chat for hours during the day, and I spent long nights in the balcony talking to him. He pampered me with his words, and I loved being pampered that way. I met him during the book fair at Jaipur for the first time. He was surely a class apart in that herd of nerds. Not at all classy or rich, but he had something that attracted me towards him.

He was always available for me and unknowingly I took him and the fact that he was attracted towards me for granted. I remained busy in my work and I could not be as spontaneous and available to him as he expected me to be. With passing time, this started hurting his ego and he became very sarcastic about everything. He wanted things to improve and I failed to address his feelings of being neglected and get better. He was hurt and I could not treat it at the right time, which replaced his sarcasm by bitterness, and we could not live with it for long.

So, even before we could think about a future together, we separated on a very bitter note. My introspection has made me realize that I have been behaving very oddly with you guys ever since. I remained occupied with Ronit and even after the sudden separation with him. I just want to say sorry for my actions and behavior which has hurt you.' She joined her hands and sobbed. Tejas went into his room and washed his face 'He is a polished bitter gourd now.' The ladies were laughing as Jiya narrated her recent collision with him, just when Tejas entered the dining area again.

'What are your further plans, Jiya? Why have you closed all your assignments and are not taking up anything new? Please let me know if you mind me asking questions. You are a grown up now and you can take care of yourself, so can you take your independent decisions.' Jiya could not decide if he was taunting. She thought of asking but avoided it. She did not want to spoil her relationship with her parents anymore.

'Papa, please, I said sorry for whatever has happened. I was uncomfortable about the fact that you tried to find details about my personal life secretly. You are my father, you could have asked me directly, and I would have told you everything. You are my idol, and your guidance will be needed always so that I can be like you. I would not mind you asking any question.' She smiled.

'My immediate plan is to work on the next book, papa. I have done enough work to prove myself as a good interior designer, now it's time to be a fabulous author. I want to explore every talent that God has given me, so that when I stand in front of him, I can tell him proudly that I used everything that he had given me.'

Tejas looked at her, stunned by her words.

'Papa, I need your guidance. I have already talked to you about my meeting with Pigeon Publishers; one of the respected publication houses in the country. They had proposed me for a Co-Author experiment sometime back. After thinking enough, I have decided to go ahead with it. I happened to meet their Creative Head last week and she sounds promising. While I was walking out of their office, I crossed paths with Ronit. I saw him entering the chamber of the Creative Head of this publishing house without even knocking on the door, and now this fact is troubling me. I sense something odd here, Papa. Can it be a sheer co-incidence to have found him there? What about what I observed–is he still an amateur that he did not even know he had to knock on the door, or am I missing some fact I that shouldn't be?'

'Jiya, whatever happens, happens for good. I suggest you focus on your strengths. Everyone has their own plans about what do they want from their lives and how they want to do it. We cannot know the plan of the whole world; also, it is not wise to invest time doing that. What I do is, I design my solid plan and make sure I execute it to the hilt. I think you too should do the same. Even if you think that you are missing something which you shouldn't, focus on your idea and keep moving forward.' Kinnary had observed Tejas mellowing down a bit and she was happy about it. She remembered the warmth she felt during the last family hug.

'I believe you would have certainly checked on everything else before choosing to work with this publisher.'

'This is Pigeon, papa, they check and choose us, and writers would die to be selected by them.' Jiya was chirping in excitement which put smile on the faces of the others present.

'Come and see me at my office at 12.' Tejas patted her back with a smile.

Jiya knocked on the door of Tejas's office sharp at 12. She knew that Tejas valued punctuality. 'Make people wait to take your appointment, but once you give them a time, learn to deliver.' He had taught this to Jiya, and seeing Jiya living up to it, he felt proud. They went through the contract which Jiya was to sign with Pigeon at length.

'I believe in you, my baby, go ahead with this. I can already see the glory of what is coming your way in your eyes. Go and live it, my love. If anything goes wrong, I am there for you. We will make sure that you prove your mettle.' Tejas spread his arms to hug Jiya. Jiya ran to him, hugged him tighter than he had imagined. 'I love you, Papa. I will not disappoint you. This book is going to make me famous and I will make you proud.' She once felt that she missed something behind the words of Tejas but ignored every negative thought. 'After all he is my father and would not do anything that will harm me.'

'Jiya, I think you should continue taking some interior designing assignments–you have your own staff and you have to help them run their homes. I understand that you do not want to distract yourself from writing, but you love that work and it won't take much from you. Think about it. These people are working for you all these years, and you cannot let them down because you are chasing your other dreams.'

Jiya smiled at him and looked at the print of the contract in her hand with affection. She finally signed it, slipped it in an envelope and sealed it with a kiss. She handed the envelope at the reception of Tejas's office.

'Suhani, ensure that you do not make any mistake with this, this has to be couriered right now,' and she walked away and called Zakir.

'Zakir, come and pick me up from papa's office.' She was still keen to make up with Zakir after the rude events of the past few days.

'Zakir, I really want to listen to the love story you wanted to tell me the other day.' She tried to confirm how comfortable he was with her after the last communication they had.

'*Jane do madam. Garib ka pyaar aur garib ki khanai, dono ka koi mol nahi hota.*' (Leave it Madam, a poor man's love and a poor man's story, both have no value.*)* Zakir sounded badly hurt.

'Are you still annoyed, Zakir? I said sorry, I was disturbed about something and I ended up hurting you.' Jiya found herself apologizing beyond a point. Zakir was hurt and she found it weird the way she was trying to make up to him. After all, he was just an employee, and there was no reason as to why she should plead so much to make sure he was okay.

'Not at all, Madamji, I am not at all hurt by your words or actions.' He stopped the car as they reached Jiya's office; she thanked him and rushed inside the office.

Chapter 11

She summoned her staff to the meeting chamber. All of them were already confused on not having any work and Jiya's changed behavior in the recent past. They were worried after hearing gossip about her getting married and shifting abroad. Other rumors hinted towards the business making losses, though the senior engineers and designers knew that the company was making enough profit to stand strong.

Murmurs, gossips and questions stopped the moment Jiya walked into the room. Unlike her usual dress code, today she was dressed casually. Somebody who was normally immaculately dressed and demanded the same from all of them was standing in front of them wearing a torn Jeans, a red T-shirt, roughly tied hair and white bellies thrown on. She looked like an interior designing student that day, but the confidence on her face and in her body language was that of an experienced businesswoman. She addressed them with a good morning. The softness in her voice changed the atmosphere in that room.

'You people have worked with me all these years. We have done number of projects together and have grown so far. I have some more dreams to chase and I think to be able to chase and achieve them, I would not be able to focus on this business as much as it is needed. We all know that this is a demanding job and my commitment to my dream will not allow me to do justice to it.'

'So, are you winding up this business, Madam? Once, in the same room when we started this business, you said that we are family and we will be in this together, always. We have never looked at any other opportunity that knocked our doors, Madam, just because we have always considered this business as our own business.' Bhavik could not wait till she finished.

Jiya sat down on the nearest chair and pressed the bell to call the service staff.

There was a lurking anticipation of fear and pain in the air, with the attendees thinking that this business was about to be closed. Where will we go? What will we do? How will we support our families? What about our career goals? Everyone was worried and somewhere the sense of betrayal was triggering insecurity in their hearts.

There was a mild knock on the door of the meeting room. Mayur opened the door and stood there with his head slightly bowed down in front of her.

'Come in Mayur.' He walked 4 steps ahead and entered the room following Jiya's welcome. Jiya got up from where she was seated, put on a hand on his shoulder and held his hand with the other, leaving everyone shocked and confused. No one had ever seen Jiya behave like this and they all were getting restless with their own thoughts over what was happening.

'Get some ice cream for all of us, Mayur. It is getting really hot in here. I am in my chamber and waiting for the ice cream.'

'Let us all meet again with our tongues sweeter and minds cooler in a little while. See you guys.' Before walking out of meeting room, Jiya paused at the door addressing her staff.

She dialed a number as soon as she entered her chamber.

'You will receive the signed copy by the end of the day tomorrow; it is already on the way in the courier.' Jiya's smile was getting broader day by day. Just then, she heard a knock on the door.

'Thanks a lot, Nitya, I will look forward to hear back from you and then start writing.' Jiya hung up the phone and called Mayur in, who placed a bowl of ice cream on her desk and left. She walked towards the meeting room with a bowl of ice cream in her hand.

Everyone was eating ice cream silently and Jiya could not stop laughing. They all looked up at her and could not decide what this laughter was for!

'Guys, please cheer up, and enjoy this treat. All I want to say right now is, please cheer up.' She raised a toast with her bowl of ice cream. They all tried to smile while they silently ate their ice cream.

The spoons finally settled in the bowls and Mayur cleared them all. They waited for Jiya to finally announce whatever she wanted to.

'Mayur, come back once you are done clearing all these. I will wait for you to join us.' Mayur shivered on hearing this. He did not understand what was happening. He quickly wound up the ice cream spread and found a corner in the meeting room to stand and listen to 'the news'. He was the one who was the least worried in the herd though because he was convinced when someone told him that it was not difficult to find another job for him being a mere office boy. The real challenge was for engineers, designers and other creative people to go and find a matching salary with all the other perks.

'It's just the last few hours that has made me realize about the highly pent up insecurity and tension in the air of this place. I have been reminded about what I said when we began to work together. Yes, we are a family, and we dreamt to grow together. However, should these facts change if I am persuading my other dreams? Why would we wind up this work? Yes, I took a break and did not pick up new assignments as I was not sure how things would shape up. Neither of you came to me to ask, instead all of you started thinking of all possible reasons by yourselves.' She looked straight into the eyes of every person in that room; specially Bhavik. Bhavik looked down, but the graph of his insecurities and doubts didn't move down at all.

'I now see the road clearly. I want all of you to believe in me and support me, and that is what family is for, right? All of you please listen to me very carefully now. I am going to write a book and I do not know how much time it may demand from me. We are neither shutting down this business, nor are we in any financial problem. What I want all of you to do is to show confidence in yourself and run this business in your individual capacities. We have learnt a lot in the last few years and it's time to run the show with individual skills. Nothing changes, except the fact that I will not be involved in everything like before.'

She heard smiles and sighs.

'Don't fear, I am not pulling myself back, and this does not mean that I won't be available when needed. Just look at this change as an opportunity to be independent and test your individual capacities. Run this business minus me, play your roles plus a bit extra of me and see the wonders. I will be available when needed, but not as always. However, this is not mandatory for anyone. Just a while back, I have figured out that many of you would have compromised on some opportunities that came your way. Anyone can move on to wherever they want, I will be very happy with the growth of each of you. We are definitely a family, but at the end of the day I am Jiya Tejas Juneja, who can do everything she wants; presence and absence of no one can stop me.' She was constantly talking giving mixed signals to the listeners. Her practice of looking straight into the eyes allowed her to judge the mind of others accurately.

'Do we have any questions, confusions or fears left in this room?' She concluded when least expected by others. She received some words of praise and assurances, some relaxed smiles and some hesitant smiles as well.

'I believe we are all set to work hard and have no questions left. If any questions hit you after I leave this room, leave it upon time to answer rather than speculating. Sometimes time is the best solution to haunting questions. It either gives answers to our questions or makes us forget the questions by sending some more critical questions.' She left the room laughing.

She could not sleep that night at peace. Her unanswered questions troubled her the whole night. 'Did we love each other? Was there any future for us?' She twisted and turned in the bed and finally she left it upon time to decide what to do with that question.

Chapter 12

She was caressing his back, and he moaned; she loved his moaning. They were lying on the bed, their backs facing the ceiling. He turned his face towards and gave a gentle kiss on her nose before he got up from there and went to the pantry.

'Coffee?' He asked. Her silence followed which he read as her usual yes.

He was standing near the platform, completely naked, knowing that she was staring at him shamelessly. His perfectly toned body looked like a statue of any Greek God. She had admitted to this many times on various occasions. His round and firm butts were her favorite. His thighs, she felt, were crafted out of marble, something she could not take her eyes off from.

'Ronit, you are too sexy; look at your thighs. I can pay anything to be close to this body every night.'

'Shameless,' he thought. He cursed himself for going this way to win his battle of rage and revenge against Jiya. He knew that he had gone too far ahead and there was no turning back. He returned with two mugs of steaming hot coffee and a plate filled with ginger cookies. She continued admiring him while he was busy digging in the word 'shameless'.

'If she is shameless, what am I doing stuck between love, lust, ambitions, money, rage and ego? She has a clear reason for being here with me in this room, and she has told the same clearly loud and clear several times. I am not even letting myself face the real reasons. Do I even know what exactly I am doing and where would all this take me?'

'Ronit, you can praise me back.' Nitya did not allow him to continue more with his 'shameless' thoughts.

Ronit almost laughed at it.

'What's so funny, Ronny?' She couldn't avoid asking.

'Does a beautiful, powerful, rich and brainy woman like you, who receives so many compliments every day need my endorsements? To praise you and to flatter you by words is impossible, miss.' Ronit stared at her with all possible naughtiness in his eyes and touched her navel.

'I know only one way to praise, you pretty woman.' He pulled her closer.

'Shameless.' She struggled to speak. He did not want her to say that. He did not want to listen to that word for his own sake. Somewhere deep inside he knew what all he wanted; his passion and madness for his goal allowed him to be shameless. He despised himself for being one though.

'I want more of you.' She said. She felt something wrong today, something different, and this something disturbed Nitya. Ronit got away from her shivering body that was wanting some more from him. Ronit did not look at her and walked under the shower.

Ronit was not her personal interest, but his failure to please her and his odd behavior today left her disturbed. She was lost in thoughts biting her lips. She took a deep breath and picked up her cell phone, dialed a number and talked for a while.

'I must compensate for this. His brain started functioning fast, and his body started sweating. Even under the normal temperature of water flowing from the shower, he was sweating heavily. This serious mistake may cost me big time. He knew that disappointing Nitya might mean a lot and he was not at all willing to even think of it. He had to think of some solid reason; at least for walking away to the shower abruptly, if not for the early ejaculation and sounding detached during sex. He knew he was screwed if he failed to do so. He started sweating like a baker baking in the bakery at mid noon in India. He remembered his house back there in India and the cool breeze he enjoyed standing in the balcony, and the way wind caressed his hair while he waited for Jiya's messages. He remembered how the thought of being with her increased his body heat, how his body sweated and how he had to rush to the bathroom to relive himself of the heat.'

'Thank you Jiya.' He whispered under the shower with a smile. He did not even know after how many days he had thought of her name with a smile.

He walked out of bathroom completely naked just the way Nitya would like to see him. Standing at the pantry platform he asked, 'Coffee?' He had already started making two mugs being sure that her silent 'yes' will follow.

'No, I am already having my drink.' A shiver passed through Ronit's body. He held on the strong shock and continued making coffee. He placed his mug with some ginger cookies on the plate and walked towards the balcony where Nitya was sitting on the floor with a glass of Chardonnay, gazing the sky. He sat next to her and offered a ginger cookie to her.

'Ronit,' She looked straight into his eyes. He was taken aback by that look.

'What I am drinking is Chardonnay. Ginger biscuit is not at all a match to it.' Ronit read her sarcasm but avoided reacting to it. She remained silent and Ronit knew that it was his chance to explain.

'Not even if they fall in love?' He grabbed one ginger cookie in his mouth and offered it to Nitya in her mouth. Nitya accepted a bite and stopped his hand finding his way to explore under her shirt.

'Ronit. Are you sure you want to go there? You don't have to do it, just because you want to wipe off stains you left on the bedspread a while back.' Ronit was not able to judge the message behind all that she was saying. He knew that she was prepared to make him look at his mistake under a magnifying glass. But he too had prepared his defense, he at least had to try that.

'Nitya, I am sorry, I could not take you to an orgasm. I am even more sorry for walking away like that. That's the worst I could have done, especially when you are doing everything possible to take me closer to my dream. Oh God, how could I walk over you Nitya, please forgive me. Please give me a chance to share a reason for my failure, and please look at my heart closer. Will you please give me an ear?' Ronit struggled with his tears, while Nitya just stay there seated and refilled her glass. Ronit knew it was his chance to go back to past and bring the best to convince Nitya to let go of this first mistake. Nitya was looking at her glass and lifted a ginger biscuit with a mild smile on her face.

'That was an evening when I was missing her very much. Monsoon was just building up in the sky and I was really looking forward to being very close to her. I messaged her in the morning.

'It seems that the sky is ready to pour upon the heated and dried sand, sand so deprived of this shower. And you know what Jiya; the land will smell heavenly as soon as the most awaited drops of love from sky will touch it. And that smell I am sure is the smell of your body.

I was sure this would flatter her, and she will wish to run to me. This could not be for real; so, I expected at least an equally romantic a message in reply. She reciprocated well but was a pathetic initiator. I waited and got disappointed, I waited for some more time and got disappointed even more. I was lying on my bed thinking about various reasons why she hadn't replied yet, just then the sky drizzled with the first shower. The smell touched my nose and I was literally aroused. I wanted Jiya to reciprocate to my message.

'Hey busy bee, why don't you fly over to me and see what is rising here just by thinking about you ;)'

I had never talked to her in this cheesy manner, but I really wanted to get closer to her that day. So close so that we felt the belongingness, so close so that she knew how much I wanted her at that moment.

She remained silent. I waited and I got disappointed and finally frustrated. I had always respected her being busy with her work. She was successful, she was social, and she belonged to a world which kept her much occupied than an idle person like me. But that day, in those moments, I needed her to cool down something in me, something which had put me on fire, and she was absent to even address that heat.

'Ronit beta, tea is ready.' My mother knew I loved tea in that weather. I couldn't say no to her and walked into the kitchen, where my parents were already waiting for me. They were talking about multiple things like we usually did over our teatime, and I was struggling to hide the excitement under my pants. My mom sensed my uneasiness and I am sure my dad sensed my excitement the way I gulped down steaming tea in a blink of an eye and rushed to my room.

I rushed to bathroom; I wanted to be with her. I must admit that I wanted to dominate her due to anger and frustration following her ignorance towards me, my needs, and my emotions. I wanted to show her that if she was pretty, I too had my charms. I wanted to show her that she would want me much more than I sought her once she knew about my charms. I thought of her admiring my body and my abilities to please her. After washing away all my frustrations under the shower, I felt like a winner. I was calm, relieved of the excitement, relieved of the disgust of rejection, relieved of the feeling of being nobody against Jiya. I had made her beg in front of me, and then I gave her everything that she asked for and much more than that; while I took everything that I wanted from her. I was sure that she would wait for me forever now onwards, and not me. I sat on the wet floor of the bathroom and looked at my phone. I swapped through her pictures stored in my phone and felt the closeness that I was dying for since morning.

'Are you all right? Shall I make coffee for you if your stomach is upset?' My rush to the bathroom was misinterpreted by my mother.

'I am fine, maa.' That's all I could say.

Ronit looked at Nitya, expecting some reaction.

'*Achha*'(Okay) is all that she said; the most difficult word to decode on this earth. Ronit continued.

'Few moments of happiness and superiority felt by self-pleasure backfired. I felt more horrible, disgusted and frustrated. What was I doing with Jiya? Were we heading somewhere, or was I just a medium of entertainment for her? I wanted more from her to feel desired by her. Desired, and not wanted. I wanted her to tell me that I want more of you, Ronit.' His voice shook a bit and this time Nitya looked at him, as he gazed at the sky.

'When you said I want more of you, Ronit, something sharp touched my heart. I was thrown back to a moment when I told Jiya that I was not her toy boy, who was there to entertain her during her free time. That fraction of a second made me lose it. Lots of emotions flooded and I was sure that they would find a way out through my eyes. And my dear beautiful lady, I did not want you to face those tears. Rushing away immediately was the only solution that came to my mind. But the moment the tears flowed and found their place in the gutter, I felt like rushing back to you. I wanted to feel desired. I desired to see you waiting for me, Nitya. I know I have hurt you.'

He kept the cup of coffee back on the tray, took the flute of Chardonnay from Nitya's hand and placed it on the tray too. He pulled her closer and said, 'Let me please say sorry, Nitya.'

She did not resist.

'Ronit, may you commit more and more mistakes; your apologies are amazing. They won't let me forget your mistakes.' Ronit laughed and Nitya smiled. They stayed lying there cuddling each other, Ronit looked around for his cell phone.

'Oh Nitya, look at this; you are brilliant my lady.' Nitya didn't bother to look at his cell phone.

Dear Mr. Ronit,

We have received your confirmation over our proposal.

Our team will soon communicate to confirm the time to meet our Creative Head and take the collaboration forward.

Thanking you,

Team Pigeon

* * *

'I instructed the team to go ahead after receiving a confirmation from your co-author. I knew it that you were going to apologize for what had happened. And in any case, that's business.' She gave a crooked smile while caressing his butt.

'Tighten your belt boy, your roller coaster ride is about to begin.' She pinched him.

Ronit laughed and she smiled.

'Shameless' they both thought.

Chapter 13

Jiya gulped down almost 3 bottles of chilled water. She did not know if she should rush to her father or handle the situation by herself. She had to co-write her next book with Ronit. She was unable to accept this to be true. Why? Why of all people, Ronit, in the whole world? I have to co-write a whole story with him. How will I be able to do it? This would require me to be in touch with him regularly. Oh my God, why this? She was sitting in front of her computer screen reading an email she had just received from Team Pigeon introducing her co-author.

'Not that it is new for you, Jiya. You have been with him in the past too. Fame, money and a bright career as an author is ahead of you, if you can repeat the history leaving the bitterness and discomforts aside.' Jiya within Jiya started talking to her. Her phone rang and she answered it without even looking at the screen.

'Am I talking to Ms. Jiya Juneja?' Shocked at hearing that voice, she said, 'Yes, you are.'

'This is Ronit Basu. Is this a good time to speak with you?' Jiya knew that the journey through the ocean of bitterness and sarcasm was to begin again. She took a deep breath.

'We certainly can. Please go ahead, Ronit.'

'I hope by this time, you are well aware that I am supposed to be your co-author for an improbable experiment by Pigeon. We can choose our actions, but we cannot run away from destiny's choices, Madam. I hope you are ready for this.' Ronit was not in the mood of letting go of a chance to sound bitter.

'Look Ronit, you are right. We cannot undo destiny's choice. As we are put up together one more time, let us focus on the reason, goal and what the future holds for us. Latching on to the threads of the past will not give anything to us except for irritated minds, thereby influencing the quality of our creation.' Jiya decided to focus only on business.

'I will certainly follow your suggestions and advices without the tiniest mistake from my side. You are one of the finest businessperson I know, and one of the smartest women I have ever seen. It is an opportunity for me to develop a business mind like yours.' Jiya started thinking about all the patience she would need to muster to be able to work with this man.

'Peace, man Peace! If we really want this opportunity to work in our favor, we will have to start from scratch. Do you understand that Ronit? We need to start as if we do not know each other, somewhere where we are complete strangers, somewhere where we have no past. I hope you know the importance and potential of this opportunity and you too do not want to ruin it, just the way I do not want to.' Jiya wanted Ronit to focus on what was coming their way, and not on what had they left behind. She wanted to make the best of this opportunity and was ready to face every challenge to be able to do it.

'So, the bottom line is we need forget the past, will it be okay if it is not forgiven?' he laughed. Jiya now was feeling challenged but acted calmly to let Ronit not know of the rage within her.

'See, we have something very huge in front of us, something that will change our future. It is up to us to decide as to how we benefit out of it. If you want to look at this as a battlefield, it would be completely your choice and your loss too. I am not going to waste it. You are well aware that I do not ever compromise on my career.'

'Oh, certainly you don't, and I know it quite well. I think we better start working so that you do not waste your time on me, which never seemed beneficial to you.' Ronit was not ready for peace to prevail.

'I am delighted to know that you are ready to start working. Let us communicate using emails now onwards. This will let us keep the data safe and we will not need to disturb each other at odd hours of the day, you being in Canada.' Jiya signaled him not to call her anymore.

'Oh, so you have been stalking me all these days.' Ronit felt so good to know that she was aware of him being in Canada.

She smiled sarcastically, 'We both have been emailed with detailed profiles of each other. One of the first few lines read that Mr. Ronit Basu is an entrepreneur based in Canada. You know that my work is my passion and I spend my hours chasing it. In that case, what made you think I found time to stalk you? Anyways, let us get the work rolling. I will send you an email with some plots, once we select one, we will share the chapters between us as per our skills and likings.'

Ronit realized that his one wrong move had allowed her to give a 'check' and her words felt like 'mate' too.

'You are good at romantic dialogues, so you may contribute with that, and I will look after the remaining parts. Please be patient till you receive my email.' She took charge of the assignment in a while; while Ronit gathered pieces of his broken ego.

'Good luck to you, lady.' Ronit hung up.

Jiya gulped one more bottle of chilled water. She realised that it was a time to take a break from everything. It was a time to go back to square one. She remembered her own words, she told Ronit. 'Let's go there, Jiya.' Jiya within Jiya shouted.

* * *

Zakir was driving and Jiya again sat in the front seat. Zakir would never ask her, 'where?' He knew that she will tell him. Suddenly she removed her bellies, turned around and rested her head on the dashboard.

'Zakir, please speed up.' She said with closed eyes.

He accelerated without even looking at her.

Dawn was breaking when she opened her eyes and looked out of the window.

'Let us stop somewhere for a cup of tea.'

'Sure, madam'

'Zakir, will you please share with me the untold story that I missed last time because of my rudeness?'

'I don't mind sharing it, but it is not so powerful that would help you to write your next one.' A hot sip of tea burnt her lips.

This made Jiya ashamed of herself. Was this the way people perceived her? Why should they not? She had given all the reason to be looked as Tejas Juneja's daughter. Others felt that their blood group was B+, as in 'Business Positive'. Tejas felt proud of this fact and Jiya followed him. They carried arrogance, shrewdness and self-centered approach in their blood. It was all about profits and benefits, and Jiya never bothered to know how it made others feel.

She looked at him. 'So you think I am interested in your story because that will help me to write one?'

'What else could be the reason, Madam? That day you were disturbed, and you asked me a personal question. By the time I got prepared to share my story, you changed your mood and my story was no more important. Today again you are keenly interested, so maybe you see some potential there.' He did not sound caustic to Jiya, but she pitied herself for being known as a heartless businesswoman.

'Zakir, I will drive back, you sit next to me and tell me your story.' He was baffled with the idea.

'Did I hear you correctly, Madam?'

'Yes, you heard me absolutely correctly. Now let us get going.' She said holding the steering. Zakir was right, his love story was nothing special to get written about, but his emotions involved were super special and Jiya felt them in each word.

Jiya wondered how every heart must be holding a story within that was waiting to be shared with someone or to die holding it as a deep secret within. Zakir sounded weak and Jiya felt like giving him a hug to console him. She realised her mellowness starting to dominate her senses and remembered how good Ronit had made her feel.

'Drink some cold water, the bottle is just next to you in the car door.' Jiya wanted to know if he had more to share.

'Zakir, I did not want to listen to your story for my personal benefits,' she smiled warmly and dropped the idea of hugging him. It has been recently that I am experiencing the soft and mellow side of me again, I should not get carried away about everything that needs emotions, it may backfire. She caught herself almost laughing. I am not very different from papa's B+ at all. I am sure that it is the best way to survive and climb the ladders of success and that matters a lot to me. She spoke to herself again. After dropping Zakir at the office, she drove back home. She passed fake smiles and hug to Kinnari and Sita. She was struggling with a lot of thoughts as to how to handle the situation with Ronit. She was also oscillating between the idea of whether to be a clone of Tejas or to allow herself to be mellower. She did not want these two females to hit the 'what happened' zone, which she was sure would invite trouble. She faked a little more during dinner and bought some peace for herself. She wound up dinner and rushed to her room to plunge in her all-time favorite corner – her bathroom. The bathtub was filling with warm water; she added her favorite aroma oil and waited for tub to be filled to a level she liked. Just then she heard a knock on the door, she could fool the ladies, but not the man in the house.

'I know everything is not all right. Tell me what is troubling you, Ginnie. Let us sort it out. I want you to focus on your dreams, away from every hurdle.'

'Yes, everything is not all right, papa and I am sure that you are there with me, but I want to manage it on my own. You got to believe me that I will sort it completely. I am your blood and we are Junejas.' She passed him a light hug and a peck on his cheeks. He patted her shoulder lightly and left. She ran to the welcoming confines of the tub.

She stayed dipped in the tub until wrinkles appeared on her skin, shouting for a rescue. She knew that a dip is the best rescue whenever she had to stay off from everything around and stay focused on only one thing. She remembered some very romantic chats exchanged with Ronit during such long dips. She shrugged away all those thoughts and reminded herself of the decision once made. She wore her pajamas and t-shirt and threw herself on bed. 'Time to do some work, girl.' She pulled her laptop close with a jerk.

Few hours of digging, brain storming, phone calls and joining the dots brought her joy of being close to solving a puzzle. Her face was glowing more with the joy of what was coming her way and the way she was ready to face it. She continued smiling until it hurt her cheeks. She turned the lights off and slipped under her comforter and drifted off to sleep peacefully.

Next morning Tejas raised his water goblet towards Jiya offering her cheers. The twinkle in her eyes was not hidden from his sharp eyes.

'You are my girl.' He said.

'How sharp this man is, do I even know him enough?' Jiya thought as she raised her coffee mug responding back to his gesture.

She was sitting in her chamber and was glad that most of her team took her decision positively. She could see them working hard with their own reasons to do so, not that it mattered too much to her. Being sure off her business being on auto pilot mode, she got her hands on her reason to smile and shine.

She drafted and email, read it thrice, stared at her laptop screen for little longer than normal, a corrupt smile flashed on her face and she pressed the send button.

Dear Mr. Ronit,

I am glad to have you as a collaborator to co-write by Pigeon Publishing House.

I thank you for the courteous ice breaking call. It was a pleasure to know more of you. I am sure we will have a fabulous experience working together to match the faith shown in us.

I believe that it is once in a life-time opportunity for me at this stage of my life and would like to believe that you too might have your evaluation for yourself in the context to the potential of this book in your life.

I promise my best to Pigeon for creating such strong platform for amateur writers, to Miss Nitya for believing in me and to you too as my co-author.

Best Regards,

Jiya Juneja

Copy of this was marked to Nitya too.

Chapter 14

'What is happening these days, Nitya?' Ronit found himself being dominated and he was not happy with it all.

'I suppose you are talking about Jiya's email! You've got to handle it. I have done my bit, and I cannot be running after all of it forever. Look at the way she has taken things in her stride, how do I stop her? Choose one of the plots from all the ones she has sent and send it for approval.' Nitya was talking like a real businesswoman, triggering anxiety in Ronit.

'See how prepared she is, Ronit. I see passion and dedication in her. It was your plan and I am sure you are more prepared than her. It is your game and I have set it the way you wanted it. Good luck to you.' Ronit heard something alarming in Nitya's words and more so the way she said those.

'What did Nitya mean by it? Will she not help me further? Will she not support me anymore? Is it going to be just my game now on? Will Nitya not stand by me for turning things in my favor?' Ronit stood clueless.

'Baby, it is our dream. To create something like unparalleled, to create something that will change our careers, to create something that allow us to work together.' Ronit wanted her to give him one sign that she was there with him in this journey- 'journey of revenge'.

'Listen Ronit, my career is not just about one book; yours could be. You had a reason, you had a plan, and we had a barter working for us. I did everything that I was supposed to do in return of your availability. Now the ball is in your court and you will have to play and win it on your merits. I too am answerable to Pigeon at the end of the day, and I cannot afford to go wrong.' Nitya was in no mood to carry this conversation further.

'What are you saying, Nitya? What services?' Ronit's voice shook.

'Ronit you have got this offer just by your *below the belt* skills. I suggest you revisit the past and recall things as they happened. It is high time that you work upon everything that you will need to steal this show. This is all I can tell you Ronit. She has got balls in addition to talent. This won't be easy.' She hung up.

Ronit wanted to cry, whether out of fear, anger or disappointment; he couldn't decide. He felt like waking up on an unknown island, knowing that all his resources were lost, and the captain of the ship had decided not to wait for him anymore.

'Bitch, bitch, bitch!' His mind screamed. He was unable to handle rage for Jiya, more than the fact that Nitya would not be with him anymore. He had put everything that mattered to him at stake to win this battle against Jiya. The feeling of being ignored, not valued and being inferior was running in his blood like poison – it did not kill him, but also made him live with pain that never let him sleep.

Ronit found himself walking away from all his morals and values to get rid of the fire of that poisoned his insides. Coming to Canada meant leaving his country and parents behind, which was not actually acceptable to him before Jiya hurt him unknowingly ignoring his passionate emotions. The means and efforts he had to undertake to please Nitya assured him that he was set to call it a war against Jiya. Jiya was not just another girl–she was loaded with brains and was a member of a rich and powerful family. He was aware of how difficult and challenging it would be. When he left India, he intended to settle far away from her and have a life that would let him make more money and find peace.

But one day he happened to meet Nitya. His innocence and other charms which prompted Jiya to look at him with deep interest became the reason for Nitya to do so too, at least he thought so. His interest in Nitya had different reasons and he was ready to face whatever it may mean. He had talked to Nitya transparently about what he wanted so that her support does not vanish in future. An idea about co-authoring a book, which would certainly influence Jiya, especially it coming from Pigeon was a deeply thought plan. After a few interesting meetings with Ronit, Nitya had talked to her team to execute the idea and instructed to prepare a list of authors to be approached.

'Ronit, once this will be on floor, neither I nor my team will ever force Jiya to be part of it, and also at any point in time later, if you will step out, I will not wait for you to complete the project. This will be completely professional – even for me. Your assured selection is a reward to these wonderful nights, and efforts to have Jiya on the list will be a further reward to many such nights we will be living.' She had said one night lying next to him.

Every day he waited for Jiya's reply. Every day came as a challenge as wait would make him go through same repulsion of rejection once again. He wondered how many more days of wait and how many more nights with Nitya to finally find Jiya's reply? Nitya was now a regular visitor to him. He felt trapped at times. 'What if Jiya will not revert? What if even Pigeon will not excite her enough?' His brain played all such questions, but he believed that his wait would pay.

Finally, when Jiya was hooked in, he was elated. He found all his compromises meaningful and fertile. He was very excited to execute his further moves. He wanted to see Jiya getting humiliated and helpless; and more so he wanted to feel happiness of being the reason behind that state of hers.

Just a night before he was walking like a lion in the jungle and right now, he felt being caged. He was not able to find a way out to avoid being tamed again.

'I cannot afford to lose this at all. I have put everything on stake. If this will not work, what will I do? Where will I go?' Ronit found himself breaking into pieces. Clueless, he decided to choose the best possible plot from Jiya's list and get working. He was nervous about the statements Nitya had recently made. He remembered her telling him all these even when he tried to talk to her about this assignment when they shared their bed. Talking about work on bed was not her preference, but he knew that it was the best time to make her commit to something; a content woman wouldn't say 'no'.

He could not find a solution but all he knew he needed to do was to hang on. His failure would mean his replacement and he was not at all ready for that. He needed to cool down and think of a solution, but till then he had to stay sailing. He opened his email and replied. In the coming days, they exchanged a few emails discussing their story and get the required approvals. In one of her emails, Jiya praised his ability to write romance which created two different impacts. Nitya smiled remembering how good he actually was and Ronit smiled with sarcasm; if I was so good, why didn't you ever praise it when I longed for it the most?

Their writing journey started, and they continued communicating on emails always with a copy marked to Nitya. Nitya read them keenly for a few days but very soon she got bored of them and stopped looking into them every day. She knew it well that she could keep a check on Ronit anytime she wanted to, but neither of them stopped marking copies to her. All this sometimes left Nitya irate, and she wondered if it was worth taking it forward. That was the day she decided to read the latest email and read the story written till now.

'Oh, if romantic stories could be written this well, I must read and print them often.' She found herself really impressed with what was in the making. If these two guys could create such wonders, why were they apart? She thought. 'I think they are this good only because they are apart, and as such this situation is the most benefiting to me.'

She called Ronit and told him that he was doing a good job. She did not miss to mention that Jiya too was doing good.

'It has been quite long since you have been here. My car, my home, my kitchen and top of all my bed is badly missing you. Shall I book your tickets for the coming month? Let us celebrate our plan finally shaping up.'

Ronit used a trump card when his persistent wooing failed.

'I am really keeping busy. I have some assignments to look after, and I suppose you must focus on your writing now. We will celebrate it if it earns success. By the way, it was your plan not ours. Good luck for further writing.' And she hung up.

Ronit knew that Nitya was stepping back but her calls were a ray of light in a dark tunnel, but this call proved it was just a hallucination. Ronit knew that he could not stop now, so he completely focused on his writing. This was really getting demanding as he had continued working for Dixit half a day and in the later half, he had to create something so fine matching Jiya's caliber and Nitya's expectations.

There were few events when Jiya and Ronit talked over phone and Ronit refrained from being sarcastic. In fact, he was much softer than Jiya thought he would be. They were sailing smoothly towards their destination and they were happy about it, mostly for the same reason. What both wanted at that point of time was to give their best to this book and live what was waiting beyond that manuscript. Without even communicating to each other, they knew that these phone calls were a fact hidden from Nitya, it was their secret.

One late night, Ronit's phone rang for long and remained unanswered. 'His ego will never let him grow beyond a point,' Jiya thought and went to sleep. Next day she found two messages from Ronit her message box.

1. 'I am sorry for having missed your call. Was not expecting any calls and normally I keep my phone on silent after work hours. Missing your call yesterday was a rare thing for me! My phone always remains

silent when I wanted it to ring the most and believe me it hurts.'

2. 'Please let me know of a good time to talk to you, I will call you. If there is anything urgent, call me any time. This time, I will ensure that I won't miss your call.'

His phone rang and he answered it on the first ring.

'I hope this call deals with at least one of the complaints that you had that I always made you wait. Her laughter sounded sweet to him.

He smiled back to answer, 'This definitely feels good, Jiya, but I have waited long, very long. I have waited for you when I have wanted you badly. But let's not talk all that, tell me about what you wanted to talk to me.' She felt good to hear his smile.

'Ronit, you know what? If you want to grow, you will really have to learn to move away from things that made you feel bad and hurt once in life. Bitter memories will tie chains of pain, revenge and ego around your heart. And believe me, you are not meant for all these. You are a talented man, focus on your strengths.'

'What did you want to talk about, Jiya? Did you call me to say all this?' Ronit tried to avoid this communication.

Jiya got the signal and discussed about the things that she wanted to. They were approaching the most important phase of the story and it needed a specific treatment. She was targeting a sandwich chapter written by him between two of the chapters she would write in a prominent fashion, creating the best possible impact. They had some brain storming and decided upon the matter amicably.

'Jiya, have you ever felt being used like an entertainment tool? I am sure not. One needs to be an emotional fool to be treated that way. Someday if you feel it, you will be able to empathize with me, till then I don't want you to be sympathetic to me.' He hung up without saying bye, without waiting for Jiya to say bye.

They emailed next updates to each other; Nitya looked at those emails, smiled and got back to her work.

Chapter 15

Jiya heard a knock on the door and looked up from her computer screen. It was Mayur who was standing there with a hestitant smile on his face. Jiya smiled at him and signaled him to come in.

'Madam, Bhavik Sir wants to meet you. He tried your intercom number, but could not connect, so he asked me to come and check if he could meet you now.' He said looking at the floor.

'Mayur, look at me.' Jiya said gently.

Mayur looked at her. There was insecurity written all over his face.

'Mayur, you are doing your work and you do it proudly. Why should you look at the floor while talking to me? Don't you see yourself as invaluable to the company? Tell Bhavik to meet me after an hour. She kept the receiver of her intercom back on cradle and looked back at the flashing screen of her computer. She was in love with the story she was writing, and she was relaxed the way it was going with Ronit.

* * *

'Madam, I think I will need your involvement in this, this is far bigger than I thought I could handle.' He wanted her to look after this deal. Jiya was evaluating it with her sharp brain. After a few questions and answers, Jiya agreed to get involved in it. She had to travel to Mumbai with him and that could be an opportunity to also visit the Pigeon office. She was a little curious about Ronit's unabashed walk in Nitya's chamber earlier and was very keen to satisfy her curiosity. All three of them thought of knowing the most about the inside of the triangle formed but the facts were unseen to each of them.

Going back to her work was a charming feeling, she loved her work. 'I love to stay surrounded by words and the way they make me feel, but interior designing always feels like being with your first love.' She smiled talking to herself.

It did not take too long to realize why Bhavik thought she would be needed to handle this client. Bhavik was totally awed by the way she took everything under her stride. It was for the first time Bhavik witnessed her in front of such a client. He always thought Jiya owned that big chair in her AC chamber because she was the daughter of Tejas Juneja. Observing her just for once handling her business in the market, he was convinced that she had earned her fame and riches by her own brains and skills.

'Bhavik, you can make others believe in you only if you are confident of yourself.' Her eyes were sparkling when she said this.

Bhavik travelled back home and Jiya stayed back to visit Pigeon House the next day. She had a genuine reason this time for the visit, but she was not able to decide if she should ask Nitya directly or something else should be thought of to satisfy her curiosity about Ronit.

'I want to see Ms. Nitya.' She spoke with authenticity in her voice at the reception.

'Do you have an appointment?'

'No, but I am sure she would not mind seeing me. Please check with her once.' Influence in her body language and communication impressed the lady at the counter.

'Madam is not in the office. You may visit her later with an appointment.' She said gracefully. Jiya could make out that Nitya was not in the office; she probably was on leave. For Jiya, it was a chance to find out something that would have been difficult to find from Nitya.

'Listen, I am working on a project with Nitya. As she is not here, I need to meet at least someone from her team. I tried to reach her many times, but her phone is unreachable, and that's why I landed up here without an appointment.' Jiya sounded very convincing. The lady from the reception dialed a number, explaining the situation to the person on the other end and finally guided Jiya to Vishv, a team member of Nitya.

Jiya sat opposite her and initiated the conversation.

'Hi Vishwa, I am Jiya. I am working with Nitya on a co-authoring project, if you are aware of it?' She smiled.

'Hi, I am Vishv, I lead the editing team here. It is a pleasure meeting you.'

'I have been directed to you as Nitya is unavailable. I am sorry to have interrupted your schedule.'

'Not at all, Madam, we are pleased to have you here and as part of this project as well. We waited for your approval for long, but Nitya madam was sure that you would be a part of this project and did not allow us to give up. Finally, you are here; and we all are looking forward for your creation now.' Jiya was listening to him calmly.

'That's really kind of her. I was in town and I thought of meeting Nitya, but I could not reach her and so I dropped by without an appointment. Please continue with your work, you must have important assignments to look after in Nitya's absence. Jiya flattered him.

'No, no, it is absolutely ok, Jiya Madam. Please tell me what I can do for you?'

'I was here to have a cup of coffee with Nitya, but in her absence, I would like to have it with you, Vishv, if that does not eat into too much of your time. I am impressed that Nitya has such a confident team, and I am sure Ronit and my efforts will do wonders having you guys making the final product.'

'We will do our best. When Nitya madam adamantly waited for you even after we had received replies from other authors on our list, we were not happy about it. Now that I have met you, I know the worth of her wait. You are definitely the best. We have got to spend time with Ronit Sir too, so we know him as well. We are sure that this project will indeed be the most exciting for us to execute and very lucrative for the company too.' He ordered two cups of coffee.

'Madam, by the time the coffee arrives, I will just make a few quick calls. I will not take too long, please excuse me for a while.'

'Please go ahead. I completely understand your occupation.' Jiya picked up her cell phone, scrolled on the screen to engage herself for some time till Vishv did whatever he needed to. In any case she had found some threads which she wanted to pull smartly over a cup of coffee. This would give her some time to plan the further conversation.

'Piyush, there is a visiting card album in the first drawer of Nitya madam's desk, please get me that.' Vishv said handing over a key to Piyush. 'Bring the key back.'

Piyush walked in and placed a small visiting card album on Vishv's desk. It was a sleek album, holding a very limited number of visiting cards. Vishv flipped through the pages and found the one he was looking for. He dialed a number and got engrossed in his conversation. Just then Jiya's eyes fell on a visiting card that narrowed her eyes. She waited for Vishv to finish his calls and for the coffees to arrive.

'This coffee is going to be very interesting, Ms. Jiya Juneja. Get ready!' She told herself and started listing the points she had to dig in. The picture was bigger and perhaps dirtier than it looked till now. She was glad that she had compromised on her self-esteem and walked in without appointment. She thanked God for Nitya's absence and decided to use this chance to dig in as deep as she could.

Piyush kept a tray with two beautiful mugs of coffee, which smelled tempting accompanied by a plate of ginger biscuits.

'Put this back at the same place and return the key immediately.' Vishv handed him the card holder and a key; Piyush left with a nod.

'I am just about done; will not take more than 2-3 minutes, Madam. I will not want anything to disturb us once we lift those cups.' Both of them smiled at each other. Jiya agreed to wait silently and Vishv assured to be with her very soon.

Jiya was ready with her list of questions and was determined to find all possible answers. The conversation started and Jiya was happy with the way she was able to drive it.

'This coffee is nice, and the ginger cookies compliment it perfectly. Thank you so much for a lovely treat, Vishv. May I ask for one more cup of coffee please?

'Certainly, coffee is Piyush's specialty and these cookies are Nitya madam's favorite.'

The Mugs were refilled and Jiya's mind was filled with details which she knew she would be able to process on her flight back home. She had found a Jigsaw puzzle and solving it would mean surprising rewards.

'It was delightful to meet you Vishv. I don't know if I should be saying this, but I am glad Nitya's absence turned out to be an opportunity to meet you. The businesswoman in me says that you have a long way to go. I will look forward to seeing you again. Give my regards to Nitya once she is back.' Jiya flattered her one more time.

'I will certainly do that as she gets back from Canada.' Jiya found one more piece of the Jigsaw.

She handed over her visiting card to Vishv, 'Can we be friends? It's rare to find a combination functional brain and such sincerity these days and you are one of them.' This sounded like a cheap pick-up line, and Jiya reprimanded herself for this.

'The feeling is mutual, madam, but honestly Nitya madam is not in favor of the idea of personal friendship with authors and clients, at least when it comes to her team.'

Jiya patted Vishv's shoulder softly and said, 'Unlike other females, I am a very good secret keeper. Call someday, if you wish to,' and left with a smile. Her heart was jumping with excitement.

Her one hour and few minutes long flight meant dry throat, twirling head and shocks to her heart. She had almost arranged all the pieces of the puzzle she had found scattered on the floor of 'Pigeon House'. Few of those were still missing and few of them were not fitting at correct places but the incomplete picture was enough to leave her biting her nails the whole night.

'Where is papa?' Next day morning she was looking for Tejas.

'He left the same night you left, and you very well know that neither I would ask him where nor he would ever tell me. He said he will be back in 4 days or so. He should be back by Sunday.' Kinnary said and started asking Jiya about how her trip was, to which Jiya answered vaguely. Jiya was happy to find that Kinnary could not make out her disinterest in the conversation. Jiya was the one who answered her questions, or the one whom she could ask questions rather. Right or wrong, her answering the questions was a joy for Kinnary.

Chapter 16

Jiya was eating her breakfast in silence. Kinnary was unwell and still sleeping. Sita stood next to Jiya and touched her head; Jiya looked up and exchanged a warm smile.

'Is everything ok, beta?' Sita caressed her hair.

'Yes, Sita mata, everything is fine. Why do you think it is not?' Jiya held her hand in hers. She turned back, looked at Sita, and saw something in Sita's eyes. Jiya kept her fork on the plate, got up from her chair and hugged Sita softly.

'Sita, everything is good, believe in your kid. It is just that I am occupied with several things happening at the same time. You know how the business runs and have you seen papa living in this silence many times? While we try to do big things, sometimes it gets bigger than we had thought of, and it calls for more energy, attention and efforts to live up to it. I know you will not want me to give up, right?' Sita found her missing girl in that hug and gave her a peck on the cheek.

'Go and win the world, my love. I have changed your diapers and have bought you sanitary pads too! I love the way you have grown up, my baby. God bless you.' Sita moved towards Kinnary's room with a cup of tea on a tray and Jiya followed her to check on her mother's health.

'Good Morning, Mrs. Kinnary, I missed your beautiful face at the breakfast table. How are you feeling?' Jiya believed that it was just one of the usual mornings with headache for Kinnary.

'I am good Jiya. It's just headache, I should be good soon.' Jiya saw a bottle of sleeping pills on a side table of her bed.

'What is this mumma? Why sleeping pills? How often do you consume them!?' It was an unpleasant discovery for Jiya.

'Jiya, it's only when I cannot sleep.' Kinnary looked at Sita. Jiya lifted the cup of tea and handed it to Kinnary.

'It's not good mumma, now whenever you are not able to sleep, call me or come to my room, but no more pills. Ok?' Jiya and lifted that bottle and placed it on the tray. It was almost empty and Jiya realised that Kinnary consumed it more often than she told she did.

Kinnary sipped her tea, ate a biscuit or two and slipped under her comforter again. Jiya asked her where Tejas kept important documents; Kinnary pointed at a drawer. Jiya delved in quickly and closed it.

'I will sleep little longer and will be good dear. Don't worry about me and please go ahead with your work. Sita is here in case I need any help.' Kinnary sounded sleepy; Jiya left the room bidding a kiss on her forehead.

'See you in the evening mumma. I will be home early. Sita, please call me any moment in case I am needed.' She rushed to start her day; lot of things were waiting for her.

Jiya finished her breakfast that she had left midway, thanking God for making Sita part of this family. Just in a while, Jiya got back to the thoughts of the missing pieces of the jigsaw puzzle. She was excited to find the missing pieces, place them correctly and see the complete picture. To begin with, she needed to know where Tejas was.

'Hello Papa, where are you? This is not fair, why did you leave without telling me? I came home with a news to share and you aren't home.'

'Oh wow, Ginnie, what's the news? I am really excited to know.' Tejas didn't tell her, where was he.

'When are you coming home, Papa? I want to tell you this when you are here in front of me. I want to see your reaction.'

'I will be home in four days, baby, but I cannot handle this suspense till then. Please tell me the news.' Tejas wanted to know what the news was about.

'I think we have surprises to share papa when you are here, you will tell me where you were, and I will tell you what I have got to share.' Jiya sounded absolutely cunning while saying it.

'Jiya, I do not like this uncalled-for suspense. Tell me what you have earned, Miss Jiya Juneja?' Tejas knew that Jiya loved to be called that. Jiya did not budge from her decision and avoided Tejas's insistence. Tejas did not like her silence but kept calm; he knew his pursuance may need him to answer her question too.

* * *

'Where are you, Zakir?' Jiya did not want to drive. She wanted to go to the office, inform the team about the deal she and Bhavik had cracked, guide the team for the further course of action and go for a drive to focus on some missing links.

Zakir was home in some time to drive Jiya to wherever she wanted to go.

'Take me to office, Zakir, and please wait there until I finish my work. I want to go for a drive after that.' Jiya walked in the office building and Zakir lit his cigarette not knowing how long he will need to wait.

She called Bhavik to her chamber before addressing the team.

'I have played my role, Bhavik, you have to play yours now. This is really big, and I have cracked it not only for you, not only for me, but for all of us. Make sure you set the correct example for the team. This is the first assignment minus Jiya for all of you. I wish you good luck. Call the team in the meeting room; I will see you all in 10 minutes.'

'Guys, Bhavik has grabbed something really big for all of us. He is the same man who had apprehensions about my changing priorities, and I am glad to see his confidence and conviction for his new role. He will tell you more, but all I want to say is it's the time to prove the potential in each of you. The success of this project will play a vital role in deciding the new remuneration structures for you all. I wish you all very good luck. Bhavik will lead this project.' Some technical instructions followed, which everyone listened attentively. Bhavik loved the way he was bestowed the leadership and powers.

'Does anybody have any question?' She asked declaring that she was leaving. She walked down and settled in the back seat of the car, Zakir shifted the gears to get moving. He knew that it was going to be one more of those silent drives. Jiya juggled between her cell phone, some papers, her laptop and gazing at the sky from the car's window.

'Zakir, what do you do when I am not in town and you have no work?' she needed to give her mind a break and the easiest recuse was Zakir.

'I go to Tejas Sir's office. He still loves me as much as he did before he moved me to your office, Madam.'

'Hmm...' Jiya had no more questions to ask but she wanted the conversation to go on.

'You know madam, I looked after his cash pick and drop, his special guests, and drove him all the time. Still why did he move me to your office when you started your work? He told me that Zakir you are the most trusted man I have, and I want you to look after Jiya. Make sure she is comfortable and safe. I hope I have lived up to his expectations.' Jiya felt that Zakir was looking for some praise.

'You have done more than he expected, Zakir. The best part is you have never complained about anything, you have always stood by me with a smile, no matter what time of the day. Thank you so much for all these years of comforts and safety, Zakir.' She smiled and he looked at her in view mirror.

'Tejas sir told me the same when I dropped him at the airport at midnight last week. His flight was delayed by 5 hours, he asked me if I could drive him around to kill the time and I happily did so.' Jiya found one more piece of puzzle.

Zakir, let's stop by for some tea. Over tea she dug some more inside him for a while; she remembered Vishv and smiled.

'Let's go home, Zakir. Mumma is not well and I will want to be with her, especially when papa is not here. And yes Zakir, I would not want papa to worry about me after knowing about these clueless drives.'

'Don't worry, Madam, we will be home in maximum an hour's time.' Zakir looked into her eyes through the rear-view mirror and they exchanged silent confidence.

* * *

'Hi mumma, how are you now?' Kinnary was reading something lying on her bed when Jiya entered her room.

'I am pretty good now, but Sita did not want me to enter the kitchen, so I am lazing around here, but I am absolutely fit and fine now.'

'Mumma.' Jiya looked straight in her eyes.

'Where is Papa travelling to?' Kinnary couldn't avoid her eyes.

'Canada.'

'How do you know? Did he tell you?' Jiya was dazed. The missing passport from his drawer, and the airport drop at late in the night were the keys she had to find the lock for. Jiya wished this piece to be a wrong fit in the puzzle, but she knew that it was the correct one and very important as well. Jiya knew it well that he was not in the country.

'You know that he never tells me about anything, but I am not as dumb as he thinks, or he portrays me to be. It is not for the first time that he is gone there. I have seen his passport and his credit card bills too, Jiya.' Kinnary held Jiya's hands.

'Baby, I am worried that it is another woman.' She was shivering.

'No Mumma, it is not another woman for sure. It is business, rivals and it is about winning at any cost. Relax, your husband is yours, just yours.' She repeated the words loudly and clearly.

Her puzzle was almost solved; her head was spinning as if she had consumed weed for the first time. She was not aware that the ego and addiction of winning could be this strong that everything and anything sounded fair to win.

She left her room after settling down Kinnary and comforting her enough to be able to sleep. She now wanted someone to comfort her, she felt lonely and vulnerable. She wished she had someone to rush to in such weak and fearful moments, someone who may not help her but put a shoulder around and tell her that she was not alone.

She thought of going to Sita before dipping under the hot water in her bathtub. She knew that she wanted some warmth to balance the chill she was feeling within her, and warm water could do that for her. She dropped the idea of going to Sita, after all it was about the legacy of Junejas. She walked into her room and sunk in her all-time comfort zone 'bathtub'. She got out with wrinkles on her skin and a big smile on her lips after about an hour or so.

'Call me back whenever you read this.' She sent this message and tried to sleep. Even before she was drowsy, her phone rang.

'Hello Jiya, this would be late night there. Can we talk now? If you want to sleep, we can talk later.

'Ronit, thank you for calling.' Her voice shook. That call lasted for almost about two hours. After that, Jiya's pace on finishing the novel increased and so did Ronit's.

The frequency of their phone calls also increased and sometimes it meant increased heart beats too.

Jiya shared the news of getting a big deal for her company to Tejas when asked about what the news was that she wanted to share. He was well prepared to answer her questions about his whereabouts, but she did not ask anything at all. He knew that she was angry about him going away like that but did not know that she could be so hurt.

'Don't you want to know where I went?' Tejas could not resist asking her, and to share a well-rehearsed story.

'Papa, it is me who is answerable to you, not the other way round. You have a business spread across the globe, and I see no reason why you should be telling us about all the time you travel.' Jiya tried to show off her cool exterior but doubted if she had succeeded, but she actually did not care as much. She was just on the verge of completing the puzzle and was getting ready to earn her rewards for solving this one.

She found it difficult, but she knew that ultimately it would be a Juneja to win, she smiled and pulled out her cell phone from her pocket.

'How much more time will you need to finish the next chapter?' She sent it to Ronit and left for the office.

Chapter 17

Jiya's team was on the go. They were all excited about the success and money coming their way after completing their first independent project.

Zakir was still feeling the high because of the lavish praise Jiya heaped on him. He was also caressing the fact of being a secret holder of Miss Jiya Juneja.

Tejas felt like being on chess board playing the game with real characters. He knew that it was just about to end, and he must prepare to give check and mate to the opponent. Opponent??? He wondered.

Nitya was busy arranging for launch of this experimental project and earn maximum credits from her seniors. She was equally busy arranging some funds she had recently incurred.

Kinnary was trying to find her peace in the consoling words of Jiya. 'You husband is all yours Mrs. Kinnary Juneja.'

Sita was busy looking after mansion of Junejas, keeping her fingers crossed tightly for letting the recent happiness and unity find a permanent home in this abode.

Two people, Jiya and Ronit were busy preparing for what was coming their way on this event, which they knew would change their lives completely. They had aspirations about their writing careers, and they were not willing to compromise a wee bit on it. Jiya had a lot on her mind to do; the biggest challenge she had to face was to make Ronit believe in her.

Jiya answered Nitya's call just on the first buzz.

'Jiya, we need to talk. Is it a good time to talk?'

'Sure, go ahead. You are sounding a bit worried, is everything ok?' Jiya sensed panic in Nitya's voice.

'Ronit is also with us on conference line. We have a situation to talk about.' Nitya was not revealing the cause of worry. Silence prevailed for a while.

'Ronit, Jiya, we will be delayed with our plan. Vishv is not part of the system anymore, she has resigned with immediate effect and I will take some time to take the hold of everything.' Nitya sounded scared.

Jiya smiled.

'Relax, Nitya. I have a solution to this situation. I too am a businesswoman, and I have my ways of trouble shooting. If you don't mind...' Even before she could complete her sentence Nitya jumped in.

'Please go ahead Jiya, I am sure your suggestion will certainly be very helpful' Nitya was sounding really panicky.

'In such a critical situation, I will take the lead replacing the key person and run my show without compromising on anything. I am sure Nitya, if you will take the charge of things, we will not need to delay.' The conviction in Jiya's words touched of the deepest corner of Nitya's heart.

'Thanks for believing so strongly in me, Nitya and Ronit. Let me just sort out things and we will talk very soon again.' Line got disconnected. Nitya's conscience was churning seeing these two genuinely involved in this situation, unaware of many things in the background.

Ronit's phone rang again just after a while. It was Nitya, she wanted to assure his support in middle of this mess. Ronit listened to her, but his heart was not in it and she sensed it.

'Nitya, I see passion and dedication in her. I am sure you are more prepared than her. I wish you good luck.' Ronit after a long time used his sarcasm, but he was surprised himself not enjoying doing the same.

'Ronit, I held your hand and did what all I could do for you, when you were standing all alone clueless, powerless, and broke too. It was me who arranged everything for your goal. Do you think it was easy for me? Unlike your Jiya, neither I own a business nor is my father as rich and influential like Tejas Juneja.' Nitya was frustrated and Ronit's words angered her.

'Hey, hey, hold it Nitya. Think about Jiya's suggestion and play your game strongly, if you want to win. I found a mentor in you when you met me first, when I was clueless, powerless and broke too. But as you had mentioned in the recent past, it was barter between us; you gave whatever you did in return of my services. I have given my best to you, and I am giving my best to this book as well. Good Night, Nitya. Sleep well, seems you need some rest.' Ronit hung up the phone seeing Jiya's call in waiting.

He and Jiya talked for longer than they thought they would. Nitya said something in her call that worked like adhesive for Jiya to fix pieces of her Jigsaw. Her intentions and plans got stronger and she wanted to confirm that Ronit was with her.

'Ronit, I want to ask you very honestly that are you surely want to be with me in this? It has become very personal for me now and getting bigger than I thought of. If you want to step back, you may, but let me know your decision right now. It is a game we have been playing like doubles till now, and I cannot afford to get caught sleeping like Nitya when it is the time to go for the kill.'

'Jiya, do you remember when I told you this that I was not your Toyboy, who was available for your 24 x 7 entertainment? After that, I was determined and committed to take my revenge. I was clueless, powerless and broke too, just then someone held my hand and I trusted it. I disliked you just because you did not behave the way I wanted you to. When I heard the words that I wanted to, I felt loved, cared and desired the way I wanted to. My ideas and intentions were supported, and I found it all real until… you know everything Jiya. All I want to say is I am with you for making this work. It is personal for both of us in our own way. Let's do it.' Jiya was overwhelmed, Ronit too failed to pretend that he wasn't emotional.

Nitya spent whole night finding peace in alcohol but failed. Jiya and Ronit spent whole finding peace in words they exchanged, and they slept at peace with confident minds and calm hearts.

'What made you think that everything was under control when I visited you last? Look you chose your price for the job of my choice. I will not compromise on anything at all. I am sure by the time you know what I can do to win.'

Nitya's anxiety shot up.

The times of sleepless nights had begun, something on the other hand was about to end. Something neither of these people thought would have begun like this and was to end this way. Jiya, Nitya, Ronit, and Tejas thought it was him/her to end it, but no one knew how and who would actually end it. Days were flying in a blink and nights got longer like years. Everyone got more and more resolute about their objective.

The date was frozen for the book launch. It was going to be grand. Tejas was very closely involved with Jiya in every arrangement for the day.

'Jiya, when is Ronit reaching here?' Tejas asked Jiya over the dinner table. They were just about to eat their dessert when Tejas spilled something bitter. The ladies unaware of this undesired taste, jumped into the communication.

'Papa, Nitya, the Creative Head of Pigeon is managing the show. She must have made the arrangements for him just the way she has made them for me. I am only working on my guest list and other things that I want to do on 'the' D-day. Papa, make sure you are present there on time. I want my family to be there. Maa and Sita, ladies get ready. Your daughter is going to do something that has not happened before, and I am sure this will lift up your heads in pride.' She said filling up her spoon with almost melted ice cream and looked in the eyes of Tejas.

'Absolutely, I can't miss it love. How do I miss witnessing victory of a Juneja?' His words passed shivers through Jiya's spine.

'Now I know why people fear Tejas Juneja, what makes him a real dictator in the world of business.' Jiya wanted to shrug off the fears and focus on her aspirations. She knew that she was on right path and that gave her all the force to persuade her decision.

The invitation cards got printed and Jiya handed over the first one to Kinnary. Jiya touched her feet and asked for blessings.

'Mumma, it's the time for you to raise your head. Jiya Juneja is geared up to make Kinnary Juneja happy and proud.' Kinnary felt something very strong in her heart, she hugged Jiya and they let many unsaid words roll out of her eyes.

'Make sure Sita comes with you for the book launch mumma. Please act strongly if anything or anyone stops her, I want her to be there, mumma.' Jiya pressed her shoulders lightly, held her hands in hers, and smiled.

Days and nights followed with number of phone calls, countless hours of work, sleepless nights, and top of it all with constant confusion within the heart. She knew that she had made the right choice and did not anticipate reprisal to anyone because of it. For her, this was about a victory with a better purpose and correcting her own actions from the past.

'Ronit, don't you really have any questions, or are you hesitant about asking them?'

'The Jiya whom I knew before and today are two different people. Jiya, something deep inside of me tells me every day to stand by you. This something is much more powerful than what pushed me to be determined to take revenge against you. I would not say much, but only that I have complete confidence in you.'

'And what if I don't exactly do what all we have planned? Your confidence in me will be shattered, and one more time you will be revengeful, right? Listen I am being very honest with you, I am not sure if I will live up to whatever is planned. I may step back lacking the guts or because of many other reasons which are confusing me right now.'

'Jiya, go ahead. Please do what your heart asks you to. You will find me standing behind with a smile. And I promise, you will not hear back from me after that day in this life, unless you want to write another book with this co-author.'

They could neither see nor hear the smiles, but both knew that they both had broad smiles on their faces as they hung up.

The hall was flooding with people. It was beautifully decorated in a white and golden theme; this loudly sung songs of the class of the event. The guests included Pigeon's invitees, Tejas and Nitya's invitees and some unknown faces which were assumed to be Ronit's invitees or media people. Some unwanted media faces were also present at the event to his surprise; he knew that there was nothing much he could do about it now. Jiya and Tejas avoided crossing each other without any obvious reason.

Nitya and Ronit walked into the event together, which surprised Jiya. She had expected Nitya to come in much earlier since she technically was the Host of the event. She brooded over the joint appearance for a minute and then shut her thoughts away!

The moment of truth was just on the next turn; and Jiya was ready to face it. She looked the calmest in the room. She saw the entrance door opening; Zakir entered, followed by two gorgeous ladies. Jiya nodded at Zakir and he read thanks in her eyes. She smiled at the ladies and they read her love in that. Jiya loved the power of love. Jiya sat with them in the first row; Tejas, Jiya, Kinnary and Sita. Next to Sita was Ronit. Jiya smiled at Sita and Ronit reciprocated; Jiya smiled one more time at this innocent confusion.

Nitya took to the dais and kicked off the proceedings of the Book Launch Programme . She ensured to boast about herself, her team and the seniors of publishing house. She did not miss out to repeat how their publishing house pursued and promoted new talent. It was the book launch moment finally, boosting the heart beats of many for various reasons.

The curtain rose, showcasing a beautifully designed cover. 'Co-Authors written by Jiya Juneja.' Jiya looked at Ronit shockingly and sudden the realization donned on them and they smiled. Jiya felt completely peaceful seeing Ronit's genuine and calm smile. She leaned a bit on her seat and looked at Kinnary and Sita. Tejas held her hand tightly and wanted to tell her something, when lots of flashes started clicking Jiya, her family and the book cover.

'May I please invite Ms. Jiya Juneja on the podium and tell us more about herself and 'Co-Authors?' Nitya wound up her part.

Jiya looked pretty in white skirt suit. She was not skinny like a model, moreover some recent weight gain made her look curvy and attractive. She walked her way through to the stage in her pink stilettos with comfort and grace. Many men present there could not resist getting impressed and many women could not resist envying her.

'Thank you, ladies and gentlemen for your presence on this very special day of my life. I must thank Pigeon for believing in me and my work and making me a part of this path-breaking experiment. I cannot thank the media houses enough to find me and my work important enough to mark their presence and grace this event. No daughter can thank her parents sufficiently for raising her and making her what she is, and I feel the same for my parents. After these important and obvious notes of gratitude, I have some surprises for everyone present here; she looked at Nitya and smiled. But before that I want to thank my father, Mr. Tejas Juneja to make me a real fighter who would never give up. I want to thank the two lovely ladies present here to make me understand the real value of life–Mrs. Kinnary Juneja, my mother and my foster mother, Mrs. Sita. I have learnt the power of love from you, Ladies. I would like to thank from all my heart to Mr. Vishv, ex-team member of Pigeon for standing by me from the day I met her the first time, standing here would not have been this easy without you, girl.

Last but not the least, I want to thank Mr. Ronit Basu for being my co-author to create this book titled as 'Co-Author'. Ronit has contributed his amazing abilities to create, and present romance to create this story. He accepted all my suggestions after all the arguments we made, sometimes, he let me dominate my ideas over his, and he never lost his cool handling my long calls at any odd hours of the day. Most importantly, I would like to add that as highlighted in the book cover here, Jiya Juneja is not the only author of the book. This man, Mr. Ronit Basu, has contributed equally, or I should say more than equal in this wonderful creation. Many others like us were proposed this concept and we – Ronit and I were the chosen one. Let me tell you, I am standing shocked as much as you are Ronit, over finding my name solely receiving credits for this creation. I am sure Nitya will be able to explain things to us and clear the confusion.' Jiya looked at Nitya with razor sharp eyes and handed the mike to her.

Nitya was shivering, sweating and losing control over herself. She looked at Tejas for a moment before she looked at her seniors. Tejas, on the other side was not expecting events to turn this way. He was in this situation for the first time in his life. Not finding the need of having a plan B had put him in a situation where he was completely dependent on a sinking lady to stop his boat from sinking. Nitya was missing the count of her heartbeats now; the presence of media, her seniors and other big names of the literary industry on this episode was a complete assurance of the end of her career.

'Nitya, please help us all to understand the situation, which is making us all standing here so mystified. I am sure you are the only person to throw light correctly and make us all look at the complete and clear picture.' Nitya could not stand up from her seat to answer Jiya and continued looking down.

'Do you want any one from your team to talk on your behalf? If none of you have enough to explain, I have a piece by piece explanation of this Jigsaw.' Jiya could not resist looking at Tejas.

Nitya's boss held the mike asking for explanation from Nitya. He was not ready to find his Publishing House facing such a situation; especially in the presence of the Media. She got up from her place and held the mike in her hand.

'I am standing here as the most responsible person behind this chaos. All I can do here is to convey my sincere apologies to all my seniors, the whole fraternity and two young hearts with hopes and aspirations. I was given a proposal with the assurance that it will only remain between me and the proposer. (Tejas skipped a heartbeat.) I was impressed not only by the money involved for me, but the potential of the idea and to top it all; the proposer himself. The entire game was set up and sponsored for me by the money and brain power of the proposer. It was quite small, simple and even innocent thing when it began, but it grew bigger and shabbier with the passing time. There were times when I wanted to quit but was tangled in a way that I had to finish the game either with the king or as a pawn. And here I am–a dead pawn. The worst is we – I and the game runner never realised that we both were pawns and the game was being run by someone who we never thought as the game runner. Salute to you, Jiya.' She left the stage with many flashes and some enthusiastic mikes following her.

Every key person in the event on the dais was clueless. They were wondering as to how shabby was the picture and how much more was to be revealed by Jiya. Even Jiya was not decisive about how much she wanted to reveal at this point, but she was clear about her goal and was determined to achieve it.

'Now, as we know that there has been an error on the part of Team Pigeon, , I want to ask the authorities on stage about how and when can we re-launch 'Co-Authors' with due credits to Mr. Ronit Basu as well.'

Pigeon's Managing Director, Mr. Nikhil Khurana decided to take the situation in his hand. 'This incident is astonishing for each one present here. The History of Pigeon is very illustrious, and we have never witnessed anything like this before. One wrong person cannot take away anything from the deserving creator and the same cannot affect the years old legacy of the publication house. We ask for a week's time to understand what has happened, and we also assure the best solution for both the authors of this beautiful creation. I personally have read this book and I am sure that this would definitely be one of the most best-selling titles from our Publication house. On this note, I thank each one of you for being present here. All the guests please join us for Dinner. We soon will announce the re-launch dates.' He had decided to manage the show diplomatically and shrug of the dust from the Company's shoulders by blaming Nitya, which was not incorrect fairly looking at it.

Jiya was amazed the way Ronit believed in her and the bitterness, sarcasm and revengefulness had been replaced by confidence and respect between them. She kept her hand on her heart and thanked the power of goodness she believed in.

Jiya decided to step back on to the stage quickly. 'Ladies and Gentlemen, before we move for Dinner, I would like to thank Mr. Khurana so much for the assurance and promise made for the fair share. Sir, if you permit, may I please request Mr. Ronit Basu to join us here and share his feelings on this day, after all it is a Launch event of his book as well and it will be injustice to us not to hear him.'

Ronit walked on the dais with a bit of hesitance. He looked like a dashing man who was a little nervous. Jiya observed the changes in his overall appearance and couldn't stop smiling. She offered a mike to him as soon as he reached close to her and they exchanged formal looking hug that felt very warm to both.

'Last few minutes has made me forget everything that I had decided to say on the launch of 'Co-Authors'. I will quickly share what my heart is shouting out loudly now. I hold my own contribution in the chaos admitted here by Ms. Nitya Juneja. I was standing at a point in my life where I could not take the hurt, failure and defeat to the extent that I thought of quitting my life too. Certain sequence of events happened, and I regained many things that I had lost and started even gaining some more. Whatever Nitya has admitted may not look as innocent act, but I will not blame only her. This is a sheer result of greed, fear, agony and rage. Nitya played her bit, I played mine, and others did theirs too for our own reasons. I do not see myself as victim and Nitya or anyone else as a culprit here. I would be fine if I were to not get the credits mentioned by Jiya here. This event has made me look at myself with a new vision. I have known my strengths and weaknesses and I am sure I will never go wrong now about people, and about myself ever again in life. I would end here thanking Jiya, Nitya, team Pigeon and Mr. Tejas Juneja.' He handed over the mike to Jiya with a smile and walked out.

Chapter 18

'Papa could not digest that I was romancing someone outside his knowledge. To find that person, he breached my privacy; he found information to reach to out to Ronit. Having known the fact that Ronit was a big misfit to his standards, his ego got in action.

He was disappointed with me to have got close to a man whom he would never approve of. The idea of Ronit's guts to get close to his daughter irked him. The more he thought about the course of events, the more he got furious. He started setting his game of revenge with every thought about the course of events; beginning from me going to Jaipur book festival without even seeking his approval to my closeness with Ronit, and finally Ronit walking over me. He approached Nitya with a proposal and her getting hooked on to it turned out to be his first winning move. He kept using his power of money and fame to play his subsequent moves. He could easily guide me in his desired direction, being my guiding force and Nitya did the same with the poor soul Ronit. I saw papa's visiting card in Nitya's office in her absence, kept in her very confidential data. Vishv, a team member of Nitya shared some information to me unknowingly and then later I approached him to tell me the facts about Ronit's association to Nitya. She was already about to leave Nitya and agreed to help me to dig into the depth of this trap. We could dig into the story to reach close to where the game had started and the planned end too. I was badly hurt by what papa was up to. I was determined to save Ronit from being a victim and papa from being a culprit. I had to act boldly and strongly to be able to bring him back to us as the man of the family. I was seeing him as another person who was blind in vengeance and knew no morals to defeat the opponent. This time his opponent was me, Maa.' Jiya's voice shook a bit; Kinnary looked up to look at her and she found her smiling.

'I didn't want my father to lose the pride, respect and love I held for him. I had to win this little battle against him to save him losing on the grounds of morals, from losing as a father and as an idol for many young men who look up to him as a business idol. My father is a winner. I had to take off the blindfold of rage and ego to make the further victories smoother and reputable. I knew that there was a lot on stake, maa, but nothing is more than the rich heritage of Junejas. My grandfather built up an empire, my father continued making it bigger, and I could never let anything weaken the pillars of this empire; we Junejas are going to make it touch the sky now. Right, Papa? Jiya rested her hand on Tejas's shoulder and together they flashed clean beautiful smiles, assuring peace all around.

'But how will we manage the media, your publication house, Nitya, Ronit and everything else that was messed up that night? Kinnary was much worried.

'Money and power are not always an unfit choice. They must be used at right time for right purpose. We have done the needful for the good of all, Kinnary. Please relax and get ready for next chapter of our life.' Tejas was waiting for this new chapter for more than anyone else.

* * *

'And here I take the opportunity to raise the curtains from our latest book 'Co-Authors', co-created by Mr. Ronit Basu and Ms. Jiya Juneja. In the history of Pigeon, this for the first time that we are re-launching a book and this event itself makes us believe how special it is. We all are progressive people and willing to move on for the better. That brings us all together to welcome the new cover and both the writers of this blazing creation. I warm-heartedly welcome Mr. Ronit and Ms. Jiya to take us through this journey in their words and reveal the book for all of us.' Nikhil Khurana quickly wound up his talk without offering any clarifications of what happened in the past.

Jiya and Ronit walked with heads up towards the dais. Without any words they lifted two copies of the book covered in glittery paper and uncovered them.

Ronit lifted a mike from the podium. 'This book itself is our journey leading to this creation, and lessons of our lives. This one is to dreams, achievements and growth. This one is to new beginning!'

Jiya just smiled holding her mike and said, 'This one is to beliefs, hopes and love.'

They both lifted a copy of the book in their hand, 'This is to us; to the 'Co-Authors.'

THE END??